The Husband Thief

by
M J Hardy

Contents

Have you read:

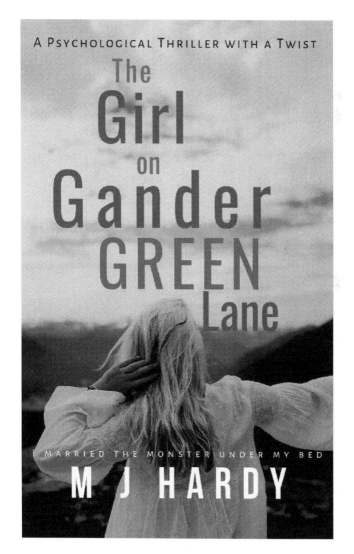

A Psychological Thriller with a Twist

The Girl on Gander GREEN Lane

I MARRIED THE MONSTER UNDER MY BED

M J HARDY

QUOTE:

Anybody can become angry - that is easy, but to be angry with the right person and to the right degree and at the right time and for the right purpose, and in the right way - that is not within everybody's power and is not easy.

Aristotle

1

TOM & KAREN

The storm crept up and took me completely by surprise. It arrived with no warning and the devastation was life-changing.

The blue lights that illuminated the street weren't unusual, there was no siren just the flashing lights behind the curtain announcing their arrival.

Like most other people the sight of them fascinated me. They spell danger and excitement and offer the promise of something different in a usually mundane life.

However, these lights were different for a reason much closer to home. They stopped outside my door.

Strangely, the first thought that came to mind was what the neighbours would think. The curtains would be twitching as everybody breathed a sigh of relief when they saw they had been spared - this time, anyway.

Briefly, I wish Jack would wake up to see this. He would love the fact that a proper police car was parked outside his door. He would stare at it wide-eyed with awe and amazement as the uniformed officers walked up to our path. However, like most little boys his age, he is firmly tucked up in bed, fast asleep and hopefully dreaming of innocent things.

I hear them approach and my heart starts banging in time with their footsteps. There is no conversation just the sound of the metal gate squeaking as they open it and the crunch of gravel as they make their way up the path.

In those brief moments when one life changes for another, I wonder what it can be. It must be Tom; it can't be anything else. He's late and his tea is growing cold in the oven as it waits for him.

Although he is two hours late, it's not unusual and there have been many meals growing cold over the last few months. The only emotion I felt before was irritation as I ate my tea alone, imagining my neighbours sitting down with their own loving husbands who came home at the same time every night and settled into a routine that only changes on holidays and weekends.

It's only as I anticipate the sound of the doorbell waking my sleeping child that I spur into action and race to answer the door. Whatever *this* is, he must be spared for a little while longer because like all mothers, I do everything in my power to make my child's life happy and stable.

I wrench open the front door and my heart beats a frantic dance inside me as I stare at the officers in shock. Of all the scenarios that raced through my mind in those brief seconds, it didn't include this. Accompanying the two police officers is a sight that shocks and yet brings so much relief I can't explain it.

"Tom!"

He raises his eyes wearily and a brief shadow of a smile passes across his bruised lips. "Hi, Karen."

His voice is weak and yet brings tears to my eyes as I move towards him, my arms reaching for the man I once couldn't live without.

He stumbles through the door and as I stare at him, the tears burn a hot trail down my cheeks as I take in the sight of him.

I gasp, "What happened?"

The officer clears his throat and says in a deep, strong, voice. "He needs to sit down."

On autopilot, I say breathlessly, "Of course, please come through."

I feel helpless as I watch Tom wince with pain as he moves towards the living room. It's obvious he's hurt and not just because of the blood and bruises on his face. His normally immaculate clothes are dirty and torn, and he walks as if each step is painful and difficult to do.

He groans as he eases himself gingerly onto the settee and looks at me apologetically. "I'm sorry, darling."

I stare at him in disbelief and not because he apologised for something that didn't need one. I stare because of the look in his eyes. My breath catches as I see that something has changed forever in those eyes. They are filled with devastation and the promise that life will never be the same again.

One of the officers clears his throat and says kindly. "I'm sorry Mrs Mahoney. Tom has been the victim of a mugging that took place when he left the railway station this evening. As you can see, he is badly shaken and could probably do with a nice cup of tea for the shock."

I stare at the officer in surprise and say in a whisper, "He was mugged?"

The officer's eyes are kind and he smiles reassuringly. In some ways, those words should bring me relief. After all, Tom is alive and although a little bruised, he will survive. However, I know my husband and this will change him. Once the bruises fade and the cuts heal, he will appear normal on the outside but his life will never be the same again.

Nodding, I jump into action, just glad of something to distract me from the shock of seeing my husband so – *vulnerable* and head into the kitchen to make the drinks. It's funny how we always think a nice cup of tea is the answer to life's problems. The standard British response to a situation that we need time to process. It's no different now as I wait for the kettle to boil, my mind racing out of control as I try to come to terms with what's happened.

The kind officer follows me in and says in a quiet voice. "This must be a shock for you."

I nod and try to muster a brave smile, saying in a low voice, "What happened?"

"He rang in and reported a mugging outside Surbiton station. By the time we got there the man had gone, and we found your husband slumped in the alley looking as if he had fought a bitter battle. We called an ambulance and got him checked out at the local hospital but aside from a few cuts and bruises, there was no lasting damage. He was lucky."

He. Was. Lucky.

Three words meant to reassure but what's lucky about what happened to Tom? He is broken; I can see it in his eyes. The man that walked in here will struggle to deal with this long after the physical damage has passed. The man I married is used to being in control and calling the shots and this would have hit him hard mentally.

The kettle switches off and the mother in me switches on. There is no time to dwell on the situation. Action is what's needed now and I must be grateful that Tom is home and not lying in hospital badly injured, or worse.

I turn to the officer and say gratefully, "Thank you."

He shakes his head. "Thank us when we catch the man who did it. We will be studying the CCTV and making our enquiries and doing everything possible to find him. Nobody should be afraid to walk home after a hard day's work and be attacked on their own doorstep. It's not right."

Grabbing the tea tray, I smile shakily. Strangely, all I can think about is correcting him on the fact it didn't happen on our doorstep but that's typical of the woman I am. I like everything done right and to make sense. However, none of this is right and yet sadly makes perfect sense. You hear of things like this happening all the time but never to people to like us – or so we like to believe.

As I carry the tray into the living room, I prepare myself for the storm ahead. Tom may be home physically, but mentally he left a long time ago. This may just be the catalyst that changes an already shaky marriage into something that has been inevitable for many months. Tom and Karen are struggling and are at a fork in the road but which path is the least treacherous to follow and will this – *mugging* - change everything?

2

SIX MONTHS LATER

"Did you lock the door?"

I groan with a longing that never seems to go away. "Yes."

My body strains to get closer to the one I appear addicted to. In fact, I just can't seem to get enough of the man I love with all my heart. My soul mate, the man I married and thought I had lost forever.

He pulls me roughly on top of him and his clear blue eyes penetrate mine as he growls, "I love you so much."

I gasp as he gently nips my neck with his teeth, desperate for the contact I crave.

Suddenly, we hear a loud knock on the door, "Mum, the door's stuck."

Immediately, I jump to attention and smiling ruefully at the man beneath me, whisper, "Typical."

He laughs softly as we struggle into our clothes and I shout, "I'm coming."

Giggling at the irony of my words, I smile as Tom pulls me back and whispers, "We'll finish this later."

The longing shoots through me again as I mould my body to his and kiss him briefly on the chest. "I'll hold you to that."

"Mum, hurry up."

"Hang on, nearly there."

Racing over to the door, I turn the lock and open it revealing the most important person in my life - our son.

His little arms cling to my legs as he says fearfully, "I heard a noise."

Gathering him in my arms, I carry him across the room and pull him into bed with us. He settles between us and snuggles in and I stroke his hair lovingly. Tom says gently, "It's ok, there's nothing that can hurt you in this house."

Jack sniffs, "I heard a noise. It was like a ghost moaning."

Stifling the giggle threatening to escape, I catch Tom's eye and he smirks. Unfortunately, I'm quite loud at times and apparently our little boy wasn't as fast asleep as I thought.

Tom reaches for the remote and flicks on the set, turning it to one of Jack's programmes that we recorded. It's not long before his gentle laughter fills the room with a lot more innocence than was here a few minutes ago and we snuggle down – as a family.

As we watch, it strikes me how one devastating moment in time changed everything. Tom and I were heading for a fall and then he was mugged.

The following weeks were hard while he struggled to come to terms with it. He was distant and a shadow of his former self and I urged him to get some counselling.

That night changed him and it's taken several months and lots of patience to bring us to where we are now - in a much happier place than we were before. It's almost as if it breathed new life into him. The man who was drifting away from me came hurtling back and our marriage was shocked into life. Gradually, he started paying me compliments and taking notice of me again. He came home early and helped around the house. He seemed happier within himself and was keen to involve himself in family life – something he had resisted for many months prior.

They never caught the man who mugged my husband and if they did, I would probably thank him. That night he gave me my husband back and I have never been happier.

It doesn't take long before Jack's gentle snores are music to our ears and Tom gently lifts him out of our bed and carries him the short distance to his room across the hall.

As I wait for him to return, I thank God for making everything right in the end. Then as he makes his way back, I can think of nothing else but picking up right where we left off.

Saturday dawns and I stretch out in contentment next to my husband. I love the weekends because we get to spend quality time together as a family. Today we have been invited to Jack's friend's birthday party, and it promises to be a good day. Harry and Tina live a few doors away and their son Jamie goes to school with Jack. They are firm friends which is a good thing because Tina is also my best friend.

Tom is sleeping soundly beside me and I turn to stare at him, marvelling at how different our relationship is now. He was always handsome but now the bruises have faded and the cuts healed, he has grown even more so. Maybe it's because of the sexy beard he grew in the days after the attack. It adds a certain ruggedness to him that drives me crazy. He is also softer and less anxious. He has learned how to relax and just enjoy the simple things, rather than racing around working every hour possible, always striving to earn more money to keep up with the neighbours.

Tom was always impressed by money and used to get angry about how other people managed to afford things we always wanted but could never stretch to. Since the attack, his priorities have changed, or so he told me. He no longer cares about other people's money, or lack of it and just wants to enjoy every minute he has with us - his family. He told me that in those split seconds after the attack, he could have lost everything and that was what worried him the most.

He opens his eyes and smiles sexily. "Morning gorgeous."

Reaching out, he pulls me towards him and kisses me softly and I giggle as his beard scratches my chin. He says softly, "You know, I love Saturdays because I get to wake up with you beside me. There is no work to worry about just lots of quality family time to enjoy."

As I pull his lips to mine, I feel the familiar excitement stirring inside. Then, true to form, the door flies open and Jack jumps on the bed, yelling, "What time's the party?"

Tom groans and then tickles his son mercilessly for daring to interrupt another intimate moment.

Rolling my eyes to the shrieks and laughs that surround me as the two men in my life play fight, I slip on my dressing gown and head downstairs to prepare a pot of tea.

We head off to the party at 1.30. We promised to go a little earlier to help out and only have to pass two other houses before we're there.

Tina opens the door and rolls her eyes. "Thank god for the reinforcements. It's bedlam here."

She laughs as Jack charges past her in search of his friend and turns to Tom. "Harry's in the garden setting up the barbeque. You could always grab a couple of beers if you like and see if he needs a hand."

Tom grins and heads off, obviously more than happy with his instructions and Tina sighs. "You know, Karen, children's parties are hard work. It's not just the endless planning and preparations they bring, it's also managing the expectations of a certain man, not a million miles from here."

Laughing, I follow her into the kitchen. Harry is one of those men who has to do everything bigger and better than anyone else. He would have insisted on the biggest bouncy castle and the most toys to keep the children amused.

Tina shakes her head. "This time he's excelled himself. We have a Punch and Judy man setting up in the corner of the garden. The party bags contain an actual Nerf gun, so you may want to hide out inside with me when they get distributed. He's also arranged for a magician to entertain the kids for half an hour, freeing up time for more drinking. Oh, and did I mention that he's invited half of the boys from the pub and subsequently set up a darts board in the garage where he will be running a darts competition, no doubt accompanied by a spot of gambling and rather a lot of drinking. Meanwhile, I have to entertain all the wives and girlfriends that accompany his open invitation and field the needs of twenty small boys who are even more demanding than the older ones. Would you like a G&T because I'm already on my third?"

Laughing, I begin unwrapping the food she bought and start laying it out on the serving dishes that appear to have multiplied on every surface in the kitchen.

She hands me a drink and I say with interest, "So, how many are coming?"

"Thirty-five."

She shakes her head at my horrified expression and takes a large swig of alcohol. "Never again. Next year I'm booking a holiday to coincide with his birthday. In fact, I'm thinking of booking a last-minute one next week."

"What's stopping you?"

"The small matter that they are back to school which involves a whole new set of problems."

Nodding, I raise my glass to hers in sympathy and sigh. "Yes, hello to all those after-school activities that require mum's taxi service. Hello to the tears and tantrums as they fall out with every kid in the class. Hello to the disapproving looks of the teacher as yet again their homework is late and hello to insanity as we struggle to get them up, washed, dressed and fed and out of the door by 8.30 every morning."

As we clink glasses, we say in unison. "Cheers."

Looking back on that weekend, I should have taken a photograph to treasure. I never knew it but if I could take a snapshot of the time I was happiest, it was then. Nothing prepared me for the turn my life took. If I could have seen what was coming, I would have booked my own holiday and never returned. But life doesn't give you a warning when it lands a low blow and I was about to be knocked senseless by what happened next.

3

"Will you hurry up?"

Already my nerves are frayed and we still haven't started the actual school run. What with rising at 6 am, making Tom his packed lunch, not to mention his breakfast and then seeing him out of the door with the usual kiss.

Then it involved waking a grumpy, sleepy 6-year-old and nagging him to eat his cereal, clean his teeth, brush his hair and get dressed in the uniform I pressed and laid out the night before. Then moving on to loading the washing machine and making his packed lunch. After that, I need to consult my daily chores list which reminds me to post the letters, leave the money out for the window cleaner and unload the dishwasher before loading it with the dirty breakfast things.

All of this while peering up at the sky and deciding whether it's worth the risk to peg out the washing to give the dryer a much-needed day off. I also need to dress smartly and prepare my own packed lunch while speed reading the notes I should have memorised by heart for the important meeting I have set up for today.

"Mum, I can't find my socks."

"Look under your bed, they may have fallen when you brushed past it."

I notice that my phone is low on charge and curse when I see the charger lead is unplugged and Tom's iPad is plugged in instead. Great, now I won't be able to charge it until I reach the office because my car is so old, USB points hadn't been invented when it was made.

It must be close to 8.35 before I manage to bundle my son into his school shoes and coat and drape his oversized backpack across his back, while grabbing my bag and the car keys from the table in the hall.

As I charge down the path, I meet Tina and Jamie heading up it and say apologetically, "Sorry, it's been one of those days."

She laughs. "Every day is one of those days. Are you sure it's ok to drop Jamie to school?"

As the boys climb into the back of the car, I smile. "Of course. I hope it all goes well today. Call me when you have any news."

Tina's eyes fill and she looks worried. "What if it doesn't work out?"

Taking her hand, I squeeze it gently and say calmly, "It will. Think positive thoughts and it will happen."

She smiles shakily and then yells inside the car, "Jamie, be good for Karen and behave yourself at school. I'll pick you both up later, so wait for me in the playground."

As I head around to the driver's side, I look back and smile. "Go - everything will be fine."

As she heads down the path, my heart goes out to her. Tina and Harry have been trying to have another baby ever since Jamie was one years' old. For some reason, it hasn't happened and Tina is booked in for more tests to see if there's something medical stopping it. This is their last chance before trying to adopt which won't be easy because they never married and Harry works away a lot. I feel sad for them because they would make such amazing parents – as they already are and I wish with all my fingers and toes crossed that they are successful.

The boys chatter amongst themselves as we start the journey to school. It's not far, in fact, we could walk, but I drive to my job in the city as soon as I drop them off. Tina collects them both after school while I work in a nearby department store in the HR department. The arrangement suits us and enables me to work almost full time, while Jack is happy and cared for. Tina makes sure they do their homework and eat their tea. Occasionally they have after-school clubs where I collect them to give her a break.

The queue to park near the school is a long one and I fear we will be later than ever today. It takes me a little longer than normal to find a space which will involve a sprint finish if I'm to get there on time.

We race from the car against the stream of mothers and fathers who are heading away from the school after having got their timing right and actually managed to get their children to school on time.

As we hurtle towards the classroom door, I look in surprise at the new face smiling her welcome.

Jack and Jamie look at the slim, petite, woman who can't be much older than I am and turn to me in confusion. The woman smiles warmly and consults the list on her clipboard. "Now, let me guess, one of you is Jack Mahoney and the other must be Jamie Sears."

The boys nod and she laughs. "I'll take that as a yes. Well, I'm very pleased to meet you, Jack Mahoney."

She turns to Jack and shakes his hand formally and then winks at Jamie as she smiles and says, "Jamie Sears, I'm very pleased to meet you too."

The boys look embarrassed and head off as quickly as possible and I say in surprise, "How did you know who was who?"

She winks. "I saw Jack's name on his schoolbag. It pays to be quite observant in this job."

Grinning, I shake her outstretched hand. "I'm Karen Mahoney, Jack's mum."

She looks at me with interest and then says slowly. "I'm Isabel Rawlins. I'm their new teacher courtesy of Mrs Batchelor who retired at the end of the last term."

"Oh, yes, of course. To be honest, I completely forgot about that."

She looks at me with interest. "I'm looking forward to working here. I don't know many people as I've just moved into the area. Can you tell me where a stranger would be best to hang out in order to make new friends?"

She smiles and looks so friendly I find myself warming to her. "Well, you could go to the local pub, The Cockerel and the Spider."

She laughs and I roll my eyes. "Yes, a little strange but quite a nice place to hang out. Most of the women here congregate in the nearby gym where there are all sorts of classes to keep you occupied. The social side is good too, maybe you should join with your um ... husband?"

She appears to take a deep breath and I see a tinge of sadness darken her otherwise light green eyes. She shakes her head and says a little wistfully, "I don't have one. It's just me, myself and I, so as you can see, I need to make friends a priority otherwise things could get lonely around here."

I feel a pang as I see the sadness within her. Isabel Rawlins is an attractive woman. It's doubtful she's not without her fair share of suitors and I wonder what has happened to cause such sadness in her eyes.

She appears to shake herself and smiles sweetly, "I should head inside. These children won't teach themselves. It was lovely to meet you Mrs Mahoney."

"Please, call me Karen. You know, if ever you need anything please let me know. I would be happy to help."

She nods. "Thank you, I may take you up on that offer."

As she heads inside, I feel sorry for her. It must feel strange being in a new town all alone.

However, I don't have time to think about the new teacher or I'll be late for work. So, almost as quickly as I arrived at the school, I leave it and brave the morning traffic heading into town.

4

Life hurtles along at supersonic speed as usual and things carry on as normal. The only unusual thing to happen is a note from the school that I find at the bottom of Jack's bag. It simply asks for me to arrange a meeting with Miss Rawlins along with my husband.

I look across to Jack who is learning his spellings with Tom and say, "Honey, why do you think Miss Rawlins wants to see us, did something happen at school?"

Tom looks up sharply and Jack shrugs. "I don't think so. She gave everyone one."

Feeling slightly better, I look at Tom. "When shall I arrange it for?"

He sighs. "I'm not sure when I can make it. Work is so busy, and it's the year-end audit. Maybe you should go alone."

Feeling a prickle of irritation, I stare at him for longer than necessary and he sighs. "I'm sorry, Karen but work has to take priority at the moment."

I answer sharply, "What even above your own son?"

Tom throws me a warning look and I turn away. He's right, I shouldn't have said that in front of Jack. It's not fair. I feel him behind me and he says softly, "Listen, it's obviously just something going out to all parents. Go and see what it's about and if necessary, I'll arrange to see her. It may be nothing and I really need to put the hours in, after all, that holiday in Greece won't pay for itself."

I nod and sigh heavily. "You're probably right, it does appear to be a general request. If it's anything you need to know I'll give you a call."

"Mum, can I play on the Xbox?"

"Have you done your homework?"

"Yes, mum."

"Go on then but only until dinner's ready. You've got thirty minutes."

Jack races off and Tom wraps his arms around my waist, pulling me close. "I'm sorry, honey. I hate letting you down."

Reaching up, I stroke his face lovingly. "You could never let me down, darling."

As we share a kiss, at that moment, I believe every word I said.

When I drop the boys off the next day, I see Isabel in the distance and head over.

She smiles as she sees me coming. "Karen. How lovely to see you."

"You too, Isabel. I hope you're settling in ok."

28

She smiles happily. "I love it here. The staff are so friendly and the children mostly well-behaved."

She grins. "I would worry if they were always well behaved, because that's just not natural."

The bell rings and she makes to leave so I say quickly, "Oh, I just wanted to arrange the meeting with you that you requested."

She smiles. "Great. I have some slots available this evening if they suit. Hm, let me see."

She consults her usual clipboard and jabs her finger on a vacant line. "How does 7.30 suit you?"

"That's fine, thank you."

She pencils me in and then says lightly, "May I ask your husband's name so I don't call him Mr Mahoney all evening?"

I feel my face flush and say awkwardly, "I'm sorry but Tom can't make it. Things are hectic at work and he asked if I would come on my own. I hope that's ok."

I'm slightly taken aback when her eyes flash and a hint of steel creeps into her voice as she says tightly, "I would appreciate his attendance but if he's too busy, I quite understand."

Something about the change in her unnerves me. The normally mild-mannered, butter wouldn't melt, teacher is a force to be reckoned with and for some reason, it annoys me. So, I adopt the same tone and say firmly, "No, I'm sorry but you'll have to make do with me this time. I'll pass on any comments and if necessary, he can make an appointment to see you himself."

She shrugs and turns away saying, "No problem. I'll see you later."

As I head back to the car, I feel unsettled. That was odd. She seemed so angry over something so mundane. Maybe something has happened regarding Jack and she needs us both there.

Grabbing my phone, I call Tina who answers on the third ring. *"Hey, Karen, is everything ok?"*

I don't miss the anxiety in her voice and quickly reassure her. "Everything's fine. The boys are in class but I just wondered if you could mind Jack for me later. I have a meeting with Miss Rawlins at 7.30 and Tom's going to be late."

She says quickly, *"Of course. It's no problem, maybe you can return the favour tomorrow. Harry and I are booked in at 6.30."*

"Of course. Do you know what it's all about? I mean, parent's evening is usually towards the end of term. This is unusual, don't you think?"

"Not really. I'm guessing she just wants to get to know the student's parents. I'm sure it's nothing."

I relax a little. "Yes, of course, you're probably right. Anyway, I should get off to work, thanks, Tina."

I make to end the call and she says quickly, *"Listen, I'll just keep Jack here after school. It isn't worth me bringing him home for an hour or so. Take the time to grab some 'me time' before the dreaded meeting."*

"Thanks, Tina, you're an Angel."

She laughs softly. *"Takes one to know one. Anyway, you can tell me what it's all about when I see you. You know, give me time to prepare myself for the dreaded meeting tomorrow."*

"Of course. I'll make sure to keep you fully briefed."

Feeling a lot better, I push my unease aside and head off to work. After all, how bad could it possibly be?

5

I'm quite surprised to find the school in darkness when I arrive just before 7.30. I'm not sure why but I thought there would be other parents waiting to see Isabel but apparently not. Maybe they've all left already and I'm the last one to show. The poor woman must have waited for me and is desperate to get home.

Picking up my pace, I walk the empty corridors towards Jack's classroom and shiver as the air conditioning blasts out above my head. The whole place feels eerie and lifeless, unlike it does for most of the day when the sheer energy of the pupils could probably power the whole school for a month if it could be harnessed.

The door to the classroom is open and I'm relieved to see the light is on. Poking my head around the door, I see Isabel hunched in her seat marking the students' work and I cough nervously.

She looks up and I smile apologetically. "I'm sorry, have I kept you waiting?"

She smiles sweetly and beckons me inside. "No, not at all. Please come in and take a seat."

She laughs as I approach. "This almost feels like my second home. I spend more time here than I do in the flat I rented nearby."

I look at her with curiosity. "It must be lonely living on your own."

She looks a little startled and I shake my head apologetically. "I'm sorry. I didn't mean to pry."

Smiling sadly, she scrapes back her chair and looks at me as if wondering whether to say something and then she sighs. "To be honest, it is quite lonely. Having moved away from all my family and friends, I never really understood how that would make me feel."

"What made you move away?"

Her eyes look sad and she says bitterly, "I never really had a choice. I needed to move to make a fresh start. You know, too many memories to deal with. This job came up and here I am."

She appears to shake herself and then glances down at the notebook on her desk and smiles.

"Anyway, you didn't come here to listen to my problems. You're probably wondering why I summoned you."

She smiles warmly. "Nothing to worry about. I just wanted to meet the parents as they say and thought this would be a good opportunity. I've met the students obviously and I'm curious about their home life. I always find it can reflect in their behaviour at school and so thought I'd do some digging to see if there was anything I needed to know. It's why I asked for the fathers to come too. I can tell a lot when I see the parents together. You know, pick up on things that may make sense of their child's behaviour at school."

I feel a little nervous as I wonder what she's picked up from Jack's behaviour and almost as if she senses my discomfort she laughs. "However, Jack appears a happy, well-rounded child and I can tell he has a happy home life. I would just like to get to know you a little. Find out if there is anything you think I should know, that sort of thing."

I relax a little and smile warmly. "I'm not sure if I have anything to enlighten you. Jack's an only child and so can be a little spoilt as a result. My husband works as an accountant for a large insurance company in town and I work in the HR department of Driscoll's department store. We like to make sure that one of us is home with Jack and if not, Tina minds him, you know, Harry's mother. They only live two doors away and we share the pickup and drop off from schools and clubs. It works well and suits everyone."

Isabel smiles. "Yes, it's good to have a secure network in place."

She looks at her watch and smiles sweetly. "You know, I don't know about you but I could use a drink right about now. If you have the time, would you like to grab one with me at the local pub?"

She must see the surprise on my face because she blushes and says awkwardly, "That is, if you want to, of course."

There's a yearning in her eyes that can't be ignored, so I nod. "Of course, that sounds like a good idea."

I wait while she turns off the lights and locks the classroom door and I follow her out to the staff carpark. She leads me over to a large 4x4 and as she flicks the locks to open the door she says airily, "Why don't I drive and then I can drop you back here afterwards to pick up your car. It's only around the corner, in fact, we could probably walk but as there's rain in the air I thought it better to drive."

"Great, thank you," I say gratefully as I climb in beside her and push away any doubts. The poor woman is obviously lonely, so the least I can do is spare her an hour or so of my company, after all, she is going home to an empty flat.

By the time we grab our drinks and find a table, I find myself warming to Isabel. She is quick witted and funny and any reservations I had, appear to have evaporated as she has me in stitches with yet another tale from the classroom.

As we sip our drinks by the fire she says innocently, "So, tell me about your husband… Tom, isn't it?"

I smile. "Yes, Tom and I have been married for ten years now. To be honest, I'm not sure where that time went."

She smiles. "You must be doing something right to still be married. What do they say, after seven years they get the itch and most marriages break up?"

Laughing, I take another sip of my drink. "Yes, don't get me wrong, we've had our moments. There was a time I thought we would also be one of those statistics but things turned around for us and now we've never been happier."

She sighs wistfully. "You're so lucky. I wish things had worked out differently for me."

I'm not sure whether I should ask but the curiosity gets the better of me and I say gently, "What happened to bring you here, Isabel?"

I watch as she runs her finger around the rim of her glass and a shadow passes across her face. She raises her eyes and I see so much pain in her expression it makes me hold my breath. "My fiancé died."

I make to speak but she cuts me off. "It's ok, you don't have to say anything. It wasn't that long ago, and it's still raw."

Reaching out, I touch her arm lightly and say softly, "What happened, if you don't mind me asking?"

She smiles shakily. "I wish it wasn't the case, but he committed suicide."

I stare at her in horror as she takes a huge gulp of her wine. "It was horrible, Karen. The first I knew was when the police called. It had happened a few days previously, and they'd taken that long to trace me because we didn't live together and weren't yet married. My whole life disappeared with Eddie that night. All the plans we had for the future, all the wedding preparations and everything we were working towards, drowned in that lake with him."

I'm not sure what to say because words seem meaningless in this situation, so all I say is, "I'm so sorry."

She nods. "Thank you, it's still quite raw but I'm getting there."

Then she sighs heavily. "You know, I wanted what you have, Karen. I wanted the husband, house, family and life that two people share as they work as a team. I'm happy you found your way back because loneliness is a terrible thing. It was one thing losing Eddie but the most difficult thing is carrying on. Sometimes I feel as if a part of me died with him that night, it was the part that gave my life meaning."

As the fire crackles beside us it illuminates the face of a woman shrouded in grief. I sometimes wonder what my life would be like now if Tom hadn't been mugged. Would I be this woman sitting in front of me? Searching for closure and a means to carry on.

Impulsively, I take her hand and squeeze it, saying softly, "Listen, I know things are hard for you and nothing I can say or do will change that. However, at least let me offer you something I can give you, friendship. Don't be on your own in a strange place, sitting in an empty classroom of an evening marking schoolwork. Why don't you come over to ours on Saturday afternoon? We're having a get together for Tom's birthday. It's quite informal and there will be lots of people turning up, lots of them on their own. Maybe you will find a few friends among them."

She looks at me so gratefully I know I've done the right thing. "Are you sure, Karen? I mean, will Tom mind?" Laughing, I settle back and take another sip of my drink. "No, Tom won't mind in the slightest. He's a decent guy who loves to socialise. One more won't hurt and you do need to meet all the parents, after all."

She raises her glass and says with gratitude. "Then thank you, I accept your kind invitation. I'll get the address from the school records, what time should I be there?"

"Make it 2.30 and expect to stay late. Tom's birthday never ends before midnight so expect a packed evening."

She smiles happily and I feel warm inside. Yes, this was the right thing to do. Isabel needs some friends right now and I am happy to become one of them.

6

Tom groans. "You did what?"

"I invited Jack's teacher to your birthday party. She's really struggling for friends right now and could do with an evening out."

He rolls his eyes and sighs heavily. "Great, what's Jack going to think? I'm pretty sure when I was his age, the last person I'd want in my house was the teacher. Maybe you haven't thought this one through."

Feeling a little annoyed, I glare at him angrily. "Don't be so heartless, Tom. The poor woman has just lost her fiancé. She needs all the friends she can get at the moment and who knows, you may even like her."

Shaking his head, Tom heads outside to the garden to prepare the barbeque, saying, "At least I can hide out behind the barbeque. If you asked her, you can make polite conversation with her and that's my final word on the subject."

Jack comes running in before I can reply and shouts, "I'm hungry."

Shaking my head, I turn to the fridge and grab some ham and tomatoes. "Ok, I'll make you a sandwich but you had better eat your lunch."

As I prepare the sandwich, I broach the subject with Jack. "Um… I just wanted to tell you that Miss Rawlins is coming to your dad's party. Do you mind?"

Jack's eyes widen with horror and he says incredulously. "What… Miss Rawlins… my Miss Rawlins?"

I nod and he groans. "That's bad, mum. What will the other kids say, they'll call me a teacher's pet?"

Shaking my head, I push the sandwich across the table and fix him with a stern look. "Don't be unkind, Jack. She may be your teacher but she's also a human being. She has nobody to talk to, so I said she could come. Be nice to her and don't worry what the other kids think."

He screws up his face and I feel a little bad. I'm not sure I really thought this through. Tom's right, I would have hated seeing my teacher sitting in our family home and yet I didn't consider my own son's feelings.

Luckily, the phone rings distracting me and I'm glad to hear Tina on the other end. *"Hey, Karen, do you need some help? Harry's taken Jamie swimming, so I could come and refill your gin glass if it's getting a bit much."*

Smiling with relief, I say happily, "Then what are you waiting for, get your ass over here."

Laughing, I hang up and reach for the cookery book. I can't uninvite Isabel, so we'll all just have to deal with it.

Tina is just the type of friend you need to help you through what could prove a very trying day. As we work, we chat and it's the first time we've had the chance to catch up in weeks. Making sure the guys are out of earshot, I say carefully, "Did you get your hospital results?"

I watch as the light in her eyes dims and immediately regret asking.

"Unfortunately, yes. It's not good I'm afraid. It appears that my body has stopped producing eggs."

Her eyes shine with unshed tears and I reach out and squeeze her hand. "I'm sorry."

She rolls her eyes. "Oh, take no notice of me. It was always a pipe dream to have another child, anyway. We have Jamie and that's more than I ever thought I'd have. At least this way we know."

She takes a slug of her drink and laughs. "At least it won't interfere with my drinking habits. Goodness, imagine being pregnant again, no gin, now that would be a shock."

I laugh along with her but I'm not stupid. I know Tina would give up drinking like a shot if she became pregnant. For all her bravado, I know she is devastated by this.

To distract her I groan and smile ruefully. "You'll never guess who I invited today?"

"Who?"

"Miss Rawlins – Isabel."

She looks surprised. "What, the boys' teacher, Miss Rawlins?"

I grin and she shakes her head. "I can't wait to see Jamie's face when he sees her walk in."

"Yes, Jack wasn't too happy about it," I giggle and she laughs. "Never mind. Poor woman. You know, when Harry and I went to see her that evening I felt sorry for her."

"Hmm, me too, that's why I invited her, it must be lonely."

Tina nods. "Yes, she seemed kind of lost and I felt bad for her. She wanted to hear all about our home life and asked us so many questions. Harry was quite put out and thought she was a bit crazy but I understood."

"Yes, it must be hard coming to terms with losing everything. Did she tell you what happened to her fiancé?"

"Yes, terrible business. They never even found his body, apparently."

I stare at her in surprise. "What do you mean? How do they know he's dead if there's no body?"

She shrugs. "They found a suicide note next to the lake neatly tucked in his clothes. They had teams of divers out searching for his body but all they found were a few personal items and his clothes. I'm not sure if that constitutes a death, and she told us the police couldn't declare him dead until they find him. They're hoping it gets washed up and then she can move on."

I stare at her in horror. "That's terrible. No wonder she looks so… haunted."

Tina nods. "It's sad, isn't it? It's bad enough finding out your future husband is depressed enough to kill himself, let alone have no body to mourn over or bury. She must be feeling all sorts of conflicting emotions. What if he's staged this whole thing and is out there somewhere? He could walk back anytime and she must always be waiting for that."

The conversation stops as Tom comes in from the garden and says loudly, "I don't suppose there's a beer going? You know, parties are hard work."

Grabbing one from the fridge, I toss it to him and he smiles at Tina. "Where's that husband of yours? Shirking his responsibilities again?"

Tina grins. "Hardly. Swimming with Jamie is no holiday. Harry will probably be longing for a beer by the time he gets here."

As if on cue, Harry and Jamie arrive through the side gate and we laugh as Jamie and Jack immediately disappear up into the tree house and we hear Jack saying angrily, "Miss Rawlins is coming here, I may as well be dead."

Tom looks at me pointedly as I shout, "Don't speak like that Jack. Not even if you're joking. Be nice to your teacher; it's only for one day after all."

Harry laughs. "Whoever thought that was a good idea?"

Tina nudges him and he raises his eyes, "What? I told you I thought she was a little strange."

Tom looks interested. "Why?"

Harry laughs. "Oh yes, I forgot you wriggled your way out of that hellish evening. To be honest, it felt as if I was seeing a marriage counsellor. If she asked us how many times a week we had sex, I wouldn't have been surprised."

Tina shakes her head. "To be honest, Harry, I'd have thought you wouldn't want that statistic coming out. I mean, it's hardly good for your image."

There's an awkward silence and Harry looks annoyed. Tom slaps him on the back and says brightly, "Fancy a beer?"

Harry sighs, "I thought you'd never ask."

Luckily, they take their beers into the garden and Tina sighs. "I'm sorry about that. The thing is, Harry and I, well, you know, we just don't have time for one another these days. I think I put too much pressure on him to perform when I was

45

tracking my fertility cycle, and it's kind of taken the spontaneity out of sex. Now he looks on it as another test of his virility and the magic has gone."

"I'm sorry, Tina, we've all hit that particular rocky patch in our marriage."

She looks interested. "How did you get over it? I mean, I remember when you said things were bad. The next thing I knew you are both acting like newlyweds. Come on, was it Viagra?"

Giggling, I flick her with the tea towel and shake my head. "Mind your own business. The only thing I can put it down to is that Tom's accident made us look at things differently. He took a long time to come to terms with what happened and it wasn't easy. Gradually he discovered that his family meant more to him than work and we started spending more time together and not in a sexual way. I suppose we fell in love again and that bond brings a closeness that glues a couple together. Who knows, maybe your news will be the making of yours. You will stop trying for something that seems impossible and just relax and enjoy each other again."

She nods and looks a little wistful.

"Maybe you're right. I have been quite hard on him for a while now. Perhaps we should indulge in a weekend away, just the two of us. The trouble is, when?"

Nodding, I look at her with excitement. "We could mind Jamie for you. Just book something and

46

let me know the date. This could be just what you need."

She nods, looking thoughtful. "You know, I think I'll do just that, thanks, Karen."

As we carry on with our preparations, she appears happier and I'm glad. I've been where she is now and I know it's hard to dig yourself out of the depression. Harry and Tina have too much love for each other to give up on their marriage, and I will do everything I can to help them.

7

It must be around 3 pm when I look up and see Isabel making her way through the side gate, clutching a bottle of wine and looking completely out of place. Racing over to her, I smile happily. "Isabel, I'm glad you made it."

She smiles nervously. "Thanks for inviting me, I hope it's not too much trouble."

She hands me the wine and I smile gratefully. "Not at all. It's lovely to see you. Let me get you a drink and introduce you to some people."

We weave our way through the partygoers and I guide her towards the kitchen. As we enter, Tina looks up and smiles. "Isabel, how lovely to see you. Let me get you a drink. What's your poison?"

"Um, a glass of white wine if there's one going."

Reaching for the wine, Tina says brightly, "You know, it's good you're here. There are several single men and ladies, I might add, milling around. Maybe they could use a friend too, and who knows, you may all discover things in common and meet up again."

Isabel laughs. "Maybe. Although friendship is the only thing on my mind at the moment."

I look at her sympathetically. "Of course. I'm pretty sure you're still reeling after what happened."

She nods and then smiles as Jack and Jamie head inside shouting, "Can we have a…?"

They stop when they see their teacher and she giggles. "Don't mind me, boys, what is it you wanted?"

Jack looks down and mumbles, "Um, a coke please, Miss Rawlins."

Tina laughs. "Goodness, Isabel. I may adopt you if you have this effect on their manners."

She throws them a mini can and they exit quicker than they came, obviously keen to distance themselves from any further conversation with their teacher.

Tina smiles at Isabel and says warmly, "Why don't I show you around? Introduce you to a few other people and make you feel at home."

Gratefully, Isabel accepts the hand of friendship and they head outside. I watch their progress with interest and see Tina sneakily introduce her to some of the more eligible single men here. There are a few of Tom's friends from work and some of their friends from the football club they belong to. I'm not sure if it's a good thing thrusting a grieving woman at red-blooded males but it may distract her for an afternoon if nothing else.

I turn away and busy myself with preparing more dishes to take outside and I'm not sure why but something makes me look up and my heart freezes.

I can see Isabel looking at somebody with total disbelief. She has turned as white as a sheet and can't take her eyes off one person. As he looks up, I see him plaster a welcoming smile on his face as they walk towards him. I stare transfixed as I watch my husband offer his hand to Isabel and smile politely. She looks confused and upset and my heart starts thumping madly inside. She knows him. I can tell that from a mile off. He is acting as if they have just met and maybe they have but there's something about Tom that's rattled Isabel and I want to know what it is – immediately.

I make my way outside as if on autopilot. Ignoring the guests who make eye contact I have only one destination in mind. My husband's side.

As I draw near, I hear Tom saying, "It's nice to meet you but I should be getting back to the barbeque. Help yourself to food and drink and thanks for coming."

He turns away and I see her gaze follow him with confusion. She appears locked in a trance and I can tell that Tina's noticed it too. We share a look and I see the concern in her eyes as I say lightly, "I see you met Tom, Isabel."

She shakes her head and says distractedly, "um… yes… um… he seems nice."

Tina throws me a sympathetic look and hurries off and I take a deep breath as I say lightly, "You look as if you've seen a ghost."

She turns to face me and says shakily, "For a moment there I thought I did."

"What do you mean?"

She shakes her head. "Your husband looks familiar to me. I mean, *very* familiar. Maybe he's got one of those faces, you know, the type you think you've seen before. I mean his hair is different, and he seems thinner, oh the beard of course, but really, it could be him."

"Who?"

She takes a moment and then turns and fixes me with a hard look. "Eddie, my fiancé."

My head spins as she says the words and then I get real, of course, Tom isn't Eddie. He's just similar and because of her loss, she's seeing things she wants to.

I say a little harshly, "Well, I can assure you he's Tom Mahoney, not Eddie. Maybe he's got a double."

She nods. "Of course, they say we all have a double out there somewhere, it's uncanny really."

Tina appears with a large gin and tonic and hands it to Isabel. "Here, get that down you. You look as if you need it."

I notice Isabel's fingers tremble as she takes the glass and don't miss that she can't take her eyes off Tom. He doesn't appear affected at all, which makes me feel better. I know my husband and he's like an open book. If he knows Isabel, he's a better actor than I've ever given him credit for. He is laughing at something one of his friends says and I smile thinking there was someone out there who looked just like him. Perish the thought.

Luckily, Tina makes it her mission to occupy Isabel for most of the time and I head across to Tom and say lightly, "You made quite an impression on Jack's teacher."

Placing his arm around my shoulders, he pulls me close whispering, "Jealous?"

I laugh. "I didn't say what that impression was. Maybe she hated you on sight."

He smirks. "Impossible. One look at this Adonis is all it takes for the women to fall but I only have eyes for one."

Leaning down, he plants a deep kiss on my lips and my heart settles. Tom doesn't know Isabel, that's obvious. However, I feel bad for her because it must be hard seeing your dead fiancé's double while you're still coming to terms with losing him in the first place. I feel bad now for inviting her and putting her through more pain.

The day turns to evening and the conversation gets louder. After the drama of earlier, things settle down and, on the whole, the party's a huge success. I catch sight of Isabel finally relaxing and chatting to everyone. She appears to be enjoying herself and I smile as Tina whispers, "That was a bit intense earlier. I felt bad for her."

I nod, "Me too. Who knew Tom had a double out there?"

Tina nods. "It must have been quite a shock for Isabel. She handled it well though."

We watch her laughing at something Harry says and Tina rolls her eyes. "God knows what he's saying to her, poor woman. Harry can be quite crude when he's had a few."

We watch as Tom joins them and I relax when I see Isabel smiling at him with none of the surprise of earlier. Tom and Harry are obviously joking because she laughs fit to burst and Tina laughs softly. "They're good together."

"Who?"

She rolls her eyes. "Harry and Tom, of course. They spark off each other and are good friends. I'm glad they've got each other just like I'm glad I've got you."

I nudge her and say jokingly, "You're getting a little sentimental, how many have you had?"

She shakes her head. "A lot, however, I mean every word. I love you guys like my own family. Whatever happens in our future, let's make sure we never turn our back on our friendship."

Reaching out, I pull her close and say softly, "That would never happen. You're stuck with us – forever!"

She laughs and points at the little figures fast asleep in two deckchairs nearby. "Maybe we should get those two-party animals off to bed."

Laughing, we head off to retrieve our children.

8

I don't see Isabel for a couple of weeks and so I'm surprised when I bump into her in the supermarket. I almost run my trolley into hers and as I look up, say with surprise, "Isabel, goodness, I haven't seen you since the barbeque."

She looks a little happier than the last time I saw her and I hope that things are finally settling down.

She smiles and says lightly, "Thanks for the invitation, I really enjoyed myself. You know, I'm glad I ran into you. I meant to drop you a text to apologise for that little episode of mine when I met your husband."

"Oh, think nothing of it. It must have been a shock if he looks similar to your fiancé."

She nods sadly. "To be honest, I think I see him everywhere. I wonder if I'll ever get over this."

She looks so sad I feel a surge of compassion and say gently, "Would you like to grab a coffee and talk about it?"

She looks at me gratefully and nods. "I would if you have time."

We pay for our groceries and take a seat in the coffee shop and Isabel sighs. "It's the not knowing,

Karen. I know he left a note and his clothes were by the lake but it just doesn't add up."

I have to agree with her. I mean, if you were going to commit suicide, why would you undress?

I nod in agreement and say softly, "Would you like to tell me what happened?"

She nods. "Eddie was an amazing man. He was fun to be with and such an attentive boyfriend. We hadn't been together long, only about four months."

She laughs at the surprise on my face. "I know, it was what is classed as a whirlwind romance."

"Where did you meet?"

Her eyes soften and she looks happy at the memory. "We met online. Tinder to be precise. We messaged each other for a while and then he suggested we meet up."

She laughs nervously. "I never thought I'd resort to online dating, but it's difficult to meet men when you spend all day with children. It does get kind of lonely so a friend suggested I uploaded my profile. I did get some idiots and was almost put off for life and then I met Eddie."

"It must have been difficult."

She nods, "It was but when Eddie popped up, it made it all worthwhile. Not everybody on those sites are duds and after a while we agreed to meet. We met in a local bar and I was very nervous but as soon as I met him, it just felt right. I never believed in love at first sight until then. Now I know it's possible."

Despite the happiness in her eyes at the memory it just makes my heart break even more for her. This is devastating and I almost can't bear to hear anymore but she laughs lightly. "You know, in those four months, I think we lived a lifetime. It was quite difficult because he had a demanding job and we only managed to meet once a week but we spoke via Skype all the time. Mind you, the time we did spend together was magical and meant even more because it was precious."

I'm not sure why but the alarm bells are ringing loudly in my mind. To me, as an outsider, this doesn't add up. If I were guessing I'd say that Eddie was stringing her along because who can only commit to one day a week? I feel bad for her because I've heard about married men who join these sites to get a bit of excitement back in their lives. It's a breeding ground for affairs and I hope for Isabel's sake this isn't what happened here.

She carries on unaware of my thoughts and says sadly, "When he asked me to marry him, I couldn't believe it. It was the full works. You know, posh meal, candlelight, champagne - the dream. Of course, I said yes because I was in love with him. We couldn't wait to start planning our future and I was going to look for a job near him."

"Where are you from originally then?"

"Southampton. Not a million miles away but if we wanted to make it work, we needed to set up home together. You know, Karen everything was going so well. Eddie told me he was waiting on a big bonus from work that would pay for us to go abroad to get married with enough left for a down payment on a house. I couldn't believe my luck and was counting down the days."

"What did he do, for a job I mean?"

She says proudly, "He was a banker, in the city. You know, it's hard for them because they have so much pressure heaped on them but the money's good. He told me he was due a bonus of at least a quarter of a million pounds, which I'm not going to lie, blew my mind."

Isabel looks totally different as she talks about Eddie. Her face is relaxed and her eyes have lost the dull ache that sits inside them most of the time. My heart feels heavy as I see what she's lost and I wonder if this Eddie guy was all he professed to be. Then her face falls, and she says sadly, "I only spoke to him the night before the accident. He was expecting his bonus the next day and then we were going to go house hunting at the weekend. The next time I heard of him was a few days later when the police called. Apparently, they found my number written by the phone in his apartment and called me."

I stare at her with a shocked expression. "Were you the first person they called? What about his family?"

She shrugs sadly. "I never met them. In fact, I still haven't. There's no record of anyone in his flat other than me. No other addresses or correspondence. The officer told me it almost appeared as if he was living out of a suitcase because all they found were a few clothes and personal items."

She raises her eyes and says falteringly, "That doesn't sound right does it, Karen?"

I shake my head and say sadly, "I'm sorry Isabel, I don't think it does."

She looks down and points to the watch on her wrist. "This is the only thing I have left. He left it when he stayed over the last time and I was going to give it back to him when I saw him again – but I never did."

As I look down my world stops still. I blink and then look again before saying roughly, "May I?"

She looks at me in surprise and removes the watch, handing it to my eagerly awaiting hands. As I grasp the watch, I almost dare not look. Silently I pray, *please no, please no,* but as I turn the watch over a dagger pierces my heart as I see the inscription.

TKJ

For a second, I freeze, unsure what to do next. I suppose ever since I saw Isabel's reaction to Tom, I've been kind of expecting this but nothing prepares me for the pain I feel as I see my husband's watch that I bought him in her possession.

She says in a worried voice, "What is it, you look terrible?"

Raising my eyes to hers, I say in a strangled voice, "This is Tom's watch."

9

I'm not sure who is more shocked, me or Isabel.
For a moment we stare at each other in disbelief and
then she says in a small voice, "I'm sorry, Karen."

I shake my head slowly, "But it can't be. Tom
isn't Eddie, I know he isn't."

She looks at me with worried eyes. "Are you
sure, I mean he is the spitting image of him? I know
he said he didn't know me but do you think it was
all an act?"

I almost shout, "No! I know Tom and he can't
lie. I watched him closely and there was nothing –
not a hint of recognition from the moment he laid
eyes on you, he's not that good an actor."

An awkward silence falls between us before I
say in a hard voice, "Do you have a photograph of
Eddie?"

Isabel looks a little embarrassed and says in a
small voice, "No."

"No?"

Shaking her head, she sighs sadly. "This is going
to reinforce your view of him but he never wanted
his photograph taken. He always took them of me
and if I did manage to get one, he always deleted
it."

She laughs bitterly. "I was a fool, wasn't I, Karen?"

I look down at the watch and think about Tom and what he used to be like. Is it possible that Eddie is Tom? There's only one way to find out.

Looking up at Isabel, I try to gather whatever dignity I have left. "Do you mind if I keep this? I think I need to speak to my husband."

She nods looking embarrassed and I stand to leave.

"I'm sorry, I need some time to think about this. I'll talk to Tom and try to figure this out. If he is Eddie, I'll soon know about it."

Isabel looks at me with tears in her eyes and says sadly, "Do you want me to come with you?"

"No. I think I need to do this on my own. I'll let you know what happens, one way or the other."

I'm not sure if I'm mistaken but a flash of excitement sparks in Isabel's eyes. It slightly unnerves me because in that split second, the shy, embarrassed, sweet woman she is, has been replaced by one who looks almost triumphant. Maybe if I didn't see that look it would make this easier, but it strikes me as odd after the last half an hour. Is Isabel all that she seems and can I really believe what she told me? When you weigh up the evidence, I only have her word to hold on to.

Making my excuses, I leave as quickly as possible, clutching Tom's watch in my hand, completely unsure about what to do next.

When a storm hits, it is natural to run for cover. The trouble is, the only place I can run to is into the eye of it and as I sit in my car, I struggle to think of a place I can go to think. Some women would race home immediately and confront their husband. They would shout and scream and demand answers but I'm not one of those women.

The trouble is, there's that part of me that doesn't want to know. Things have been so good between us since he was mugged, I don't want anything to affect that. As I think back to the days before the attack, I wouldn't hesitate to believe Tom was Eddie. Could it be that the mugging made Tom realise his priorities and knocked some sense into him? It's likely because from what Isabel says, it was about that time that Eddie disappeared. There are too many coincidences for it not to be Tom but I know what I saw. I was looking out for it and when Tom saw Isabel there was nothing to suggest that he had ever seen her before.

Clutching the watch, I run through every possible scenario in my mind but can't ignore the obvious. Isabel has Tom's watch and how did she come to be in possession of it? The only rational explanation must be because Tom left it there.

I can't face going home, so head off to see the only other person I confide everything to outside of my husband. My best friend – Tina.

Luckily, the boys are at a friend's house this afternoon and I'm not due to pick them up for another hour. As I knock on her door, I wonder if I should confide in her. After all, there may be a simple explanation for all of this. Tom will be angry if he finds out I've discussed it with her before him. However, it involves him and he could *be* the problem. I need to talk to someone neutral in all of this before I go mad.

One look at my face and Tina immediately knows something's up. She grabs my hand and pulls me inside, saying with concern, "What's happened?"

I follow her into the kitchen and sit down heavily on the bar stool and lay Tom's watch on the counter.

She looks at it in confusion and says, "What? It's a man's watch."

The tears well in my eyes and I say roughly, "Tom's watch."

Cocking her head to one side, she shrugs, "So, what's the problem?"

"Isabel had it."

"Why, did she find it or something?"

I laugh bitterly. "Yes, beside her bed when her fiancé left it there."

The shock in Tina's eyes almost makes me laugh like a madwoman. She just stares at me in confusion and then says firmly, "Right then, start at the beginning."

By the time I fill her in on what Isabel said, she looks as sick as I feel.

Shaking her head, she says roughly, "Listen, I know this looks bad but can you trust her account of things? I mean, when you look at the actual evidence, all she has is this watch. The rest is just her words and I'm not going lie Karen but there's something odd about that woman. This is all a little too textbook for my liking. Do you think she's taken a fancy to Tom and is setting out to destroy your marriage?"

"But why? She didn't know Tom until the barbeque. This story was told long before that meeting."

Tina shrugs. "So what? She may have seen him somewhere before. Who knows, she may have worked with him in the past, gone to school with him – anything? I'm not sure you can completely trust her story."

Shaking my head, I pick up the watch. "But how did she get the watch? Surely that's enough evidence in itself. There is no way she could have this unless…"

Tina looks shocked. "Do you think Isabel mugged Tom?"

I almost laugh at the thought of the petite woman inflicting the type of injuries on Tom that I saw and shake my head.

"No, I don't think it was her. However, you do have a point. Maybe it was Eddie who attacked him? That would work. Perhaps Eddie mugged Tom, took his watch and possessions. He could have been hiding behind a false identity and even made himself look like Tom."

Tina nods emphatically. "That's it. Of course, it is."

She reaches for the kettle and says happily, "You know, I knew there would be a simple explanation for this. Tom is besotted with you, of course, he would never cheat."

I try to share her belief but the saying 'And pigs might fly' come to mind. The Tom he used to be would be more than capable of cheating. However, am I prepared to ruin this perfect life we have now by challenging him with this and does it matter anymore? Should I just paper over the cracks and carry on as normal, putting this down as a fanciful tale?

As Tina hands me the mug of tea, I think I come to a decision. *I am*. Rightly or wrongly, I can't go back to how things were before. I just can't.

10

Despite what I decided, it's hard. I find myself being off with Tom and I can tell he's confused. I don't want him to touch me and there's something big and catastrophic sitting between us and I don't know what to do about it.

It must be a week later when he comes home, he sends Jack off to play on the PlayStation and closes the kitchen door.

I look at him in surprise and he says firmly, "Talk to me, what's bothering you?"

I try to brush it off. "I'm sorry, I'm just tired. Work is quite demanding and I feel as if I'm coming down with something."

I lower my eyes in case he sees the lies resting in them and he moves across and raises my chin to face him.

"Bullshit!"

"Excuse me?"

He looks irritated. "I know when you're lying and this is all Bullshit. What's the real problem?"

I can't help it and my resolve crumbles and my eyes fill with tears. He looks surprised and pulls me gently towards him, whispering, "It's ok, darling. You can tell me, whatever it is."

Just for a moment, I snuggle into his chest and allow him to wrap his arms around me. I wish it didn't matter, but it does. I need to know the truth even though I might not like it. Surely, we are strong enough to get through anything life throws at us?

So, with a sigh, I pull away and move to the bag hanging on the peg behind the door.

I take out the watch and hold it out to him.

"Yours I believe."

He looks surprised, and a little confused but I don't miss the alarm enter his eyes.

"Where did you get this?"

"Isabel gave it to me."

He looks confused which settles my nerves – a little.

"How did she get hold of this?"

I shake my head and say nervously, "It belonged to her fiancé."

Tom just stares at me in disbelief and then at the watch. I can see the cogs turning in his mind and after what feels like forever, he says in a broken voice, "He stole this."

I catch my breath. "Who?"

He raises tortured eyes to mine and I wish I could rewind this conversation and had kept my mouth shut as I see he's back there at the moment his life unravelled, and he changed forever.

Sitting beside him, I take his hand, "The man who mugged you?"

He nods and I don't miss the anguish in his eyes. Rubbing his back, I say softly, "Do you want to talk about it?"

He shakes his head. "No, I want to forget that night ever happened. I don't want to think about that man and what he did and I don't ever want to see – *that* again."

He throws it to the floor and stamps on it hard and I watch it shatter under his shoe and stare in disbelief.

Then he pushes away from the table and grabs his keys. "I'm going out. I'm sorry, I need to be on my own."

I run after him but he's too fast. As I watch the taillights disappear from view, the tears stream down my face. I should have known not to raise a bad memory. He's come so far and now I've set him back.

I head back inside and try to pick up the pieces of the watch like I did my husband after that fateful night. Even now he won't talk about what really happened to him but I know he took a terrible beating and for a proud man that was a lot to deal with.

I remember the sleepless nights and the nightmares. His bruises and cuts healed but his mind took a lot longer. The man he became, dare I say it, was a huge improvement on the one that had left that morning. It almost made him re-evaluate his life, and he became the man I married all those years ago.

We didn't have sex for at least three months after the attack. He couldn't bear me to touch him and told me he didn't deserve me. He slept in the spare room and we were more like friends than husband and wife. I think the counselling helped as he began to relax more and pushed what happened in the past where I should have left it. Now I only have myself to blame for what's happened by dredging up the past and confronting him with something I should have known he knew nothing about.

In my heart, I really believe that because if that was Tom in Isabel's bed, then I'm the Queen of England.

Tom doesn't return for another two hours. While I wait, I drink endless cups of tea and sit watching the clock on the wall anxiously. When the door slams, I jump to my feet and nervously walk to the hallway and Tom looks at me sheepishly. "I'm sorry, darling."

The relief hits me hard as I walk into his open arms and cling to him.

"Don't be sorry, I'm the one who should have known not to raise a subject neither of us is in a position to deal with."

He strokes my hair and takes a deep breath, filling his lungs with the scent of my hair.

"Hmm, I always love the smell of you, Karen. Never change what products you use."

Pulling back, I look at him with surprise as I see the lust in his eyes. My breath hitches as I see something that hasn't been there for many years. Desperation, a longing and a sense of ownership that makes me weak at the knees.

Tom groans and pushes me hard against the wall. He bunches my skirt around my waist and leans into me, kissing my mouth before moving down to my neck and biting it hard. I reach across and pull his trousers down like a woman possessed, just desperate to feel him inside me and prove that nothing can come between us.

Tom takes me right here in the hallway, against the wall with my legs wrapped around his waist. It's hot, dirty and sexy and unlike anything we normally do. As he thrusts inside, it's as if we are two desperate animals mating in the wild. No loving whispers, no gentle touches, just raw sex that's over in a matter of minutes.

We gasp for air as we slump against the wall, both of us a little shocked at the sheer brutality of what just happened. Then Tom pulls back and smiles apologetically.

"I'm sorry, darling. I don't know what came over me but fuck me, that was the best sex I've had in years."

For some reason, we both burst out laughing and something shifts between us. What happened earlier with the watch is forgotten as we file it away with the memory the night Tom was attacked. The important thing is that we moved on and I make a vow not to allow it back into our lives.

All that matters now is the future and if – a big if - Tom was cheating on me with Isabel, he isn't now and that's all that matters.

11

When Tina drops Jamie off the next morning, I see large black shadows under her eyes. She smiles but I don't miss the sadness in her and say quickly to the boys. "Jump in the car, I won't be a minute."

As soon as the door is closed, I steer her away from the car and say in a whisper, "What's happened, you look dreadful?"

She shakes her head. "Is it that obvious?"

I nod and her eyes fill with tears. "It's awful, Karen. Ever since the doctor told me I couldn't have any more children; I can't seem to accept it. It's consuming me. I find myself looking at pictures of Jamie as a baby and just crying at the memories. I research alternative ways of conceiving all the time and look at operations that may make things change. Harry is getting angry and we've had terrible arguments. He has even taken to sleeping in the spare room and to be honest that hurts the most. The one time I need him to hold me and reassure me that everything will be ok, he won't."

"Maybe he's hurting too. Maybe he can't deal with it, after all, you said he wanted another child too. This must be hard for him to come to terms with."

She nods sadly. "That's how selfish I've become. I can only think of one thing. I just want a baby,

Karen; why is that such a bad thing? I'm grieving for the child I will never have and I can't move past it."

Reaching out, I hug her gently and whisper, "Why don't you both come over this evening for supper? It may help lighten the situation and an evening out will take away the pressure a little."

She smiles gratefully. "You're a good friend, do you know that?"

As I look at my watch, she says quickly, "What happened last night, with the watch? Sorry, I'm so wrapped up in my own problems I forgot to ask."

Shrugging, I paper over the cracks as usual. "It was the one that was stolen. We think Isabel's fiancé may either be the one who mugged Tom or bought it from him. To be honest, Tina, it's in the past for both of us now. Tom doesn't want any reminders of that night and neither do I."

She looks worried. "But what if it was… you know… an affair?"

"If it was, it's long since over. I have to accept that I may never know if Tom really was Eddie, but that night changed him and he is now the devoted loving husband I married all those years ago. It's not worth the grief involved dredging up the past and for all our sakes, I'm locking it away and getting on with my life."

She nods in agreement. "You know, I think you're right honey. Sometimes things happen that make everything that came before it meaningless. I think I'd do the same in your shoes. I feel sorry for Isabel though; it doesn't look as if she'll ever know what happened to her fiancé."

At the mention of Isabel, I feel a prickle of guilt and then push it away.

"I can't put her before my family, Tina and she will just have to find her own way. Taking this job was the first step and maybe in time she will meet someone else and settle down, putting this sorry business behind her. From what she told me it all sounded dodgy, anyway. What man won't allow his photo to be taken and only sees his fianceé one night a week? Who lives in a flat with no possessions and no family to speak of? A cheating man that's for sure. A man who sets up an online dating profile with one aim in mind. To cheat. Whether that's on a wife back at home or several women at the same time. Who knows, this Eddie may have several other Isabel's on the go at the same time? That may not even be his name and if Eddie was Tom, then he isn't now because Tom has proven over and over again that he's mine."

Tina smiles happily and looks towards the car. "You know, I think you're right. Put it all to bed and move on. Maybe I should take my own advice and it starts tonight. I need to repair my own relationship with Harry first before trying to bring another life into our family because if I keep on going the way I am, we won't be a family for much longer."

We head our separate ways and I think about what Tina said. Yes, sometimes we need to bury the past to move on. We may not like it but it's important to weigh up the implications of what may happen if we allow the past to control our future.

Feeling a lot happier, I turn into the road near the school and know what needs to be done next.

Isabel is in her usual place standing by the classroom door with the ever-present clipboard in her hands. She looks around her, occasionally calling out to admonish brawling children, or laughing at something a parent or student say to her.

As she sees me coming, I don't miss the flash of anxiety that greets me as she walks over and smiles at Jack and Jamie. "Hey, boys, why don't you run along and play a game of football while I talk to mummy."

They don't need a second invitation and she laughs softly, "Typical boys. They do have so much energy to harness."

I nod and then say firmly, "Listen, I just wanted to speak to you about the watch."

She looks nervous and I feel a little bad for her. "I spoke to Tom, and he said it was stolen from him. I'm not sure if you know but Tom was attacked about seven months ago when he came home one night."

She looks shocked and I smile ruefully. "It's been tough but we're getting there. The watch was stolen along with several other personal possessions. Tom believes the attacker either sold them on or …"

I hesitate and Isabel says sadly, "Or you think Eddie may have attacked Tom."

I feel bad and say gently, "It's a possibility. It may have been that but more likely it's because he sold them on. I don't think we'll ever really know because Tom is traumatised by what happened and I'm sorry but I can't dredge things up again. I think it's best all round if we let this lie."

I see the tears well in Isabel's eyes and place my hand on her arm in sympathy. The bell rings and she shakes her head sadly. "Oh well, duty calls. I'm sorry to cause you problems, Karen."

As she turns away, I feel bad and say quickly, "Isabel."

She turns and I say awkwardly, "It doesn't mean we can't be friends though. I mean, I'm pretty sure you can use one and to be honest, so could I."

Her eyes brighten and she nods happily. "I appreciate that, thank you. You know, even if I never find out what happened to Eddie, at least I can start again somewhere new and as places go, this seems like a good one."

She smiles and heads off to the classroom and I feel a sense of closure that puts my mind at rest. Yes, this is the best all around. We all need to move on and leave the past where it belongs.

12
HARRY & TINA

"Hey, Isabel, over here."

I smile as I see a familiar face and she heads over.

"Hi, Tina. I didn't know you belonged to this gym?"

"Well, technically I've been a member for two years but I've kind of let my attendance slide a little. To be honest, I just had to get out of the house and distract myself for a bit."

She looks concerned and I shrug. "It's ok, nothing too bad. You know what it's like, life gets a little too much on occasion. Harry told me to grab a change of scene so, here I am. Anyway, how long have you been a member?"

"Not long. To be honest, it's something Karen suggested when I first arrived. I don't have much else to occupy my time, so I head here most evenings."

She looks around in surprise. "Is Karen not with you?"

Shaking my head, I pull a face. "No, she's having a 'date night' with Tom."

I don't miss the flicker of envy in Isabel's eyes and feel bad. "Still no word about your fiancé?"

She shakes her head sadly. "No, I think the trail's gone cold and there's nothing more they can do. Maybe I'll never know."

I feel bad for her; it must be awful not knowing, so, I say gently, "Maybe you should try to put it in the past. You know, move on. I don't mean dating or anything but maybe take up a hobby or join a club, you know, meet a few people and find a new passion."

She raises her eyes and smiles. "I thought I was by coming here."

Grinning, I say nothing because the teacher calls the fitness class to attention and we begin the gruelling workout.

As I watch Isabel going through her paces, I feel glad she's here. Despite how weird the situation is, I do kind of like her and want things to go right for her. I wonder if she will ever find out what happened to Eddie. I hope so, for her sake at least.

By the end of the class, I'm totally exhausted and as I wipe the sweat from my face, she comes over and grins. "You're a little out of practice."

Groaning, I stretch my aching legs and sigh. "You could say that. The only exercise I've been getting lately is when I move from room to room. I think this class is long overdue."

She smiles and as she gathers up her belongings, I say impulsively, "Do you fancy grabbing a drink in the wine bar next door? I'm not ready to head back to suburbia just yet."

Her eyes light up and I can tell she's pleased to be asked.

"That would be great, thank you. To be honest, it's quite lonely living on your own in a strange town. I would love to."

As we head next door, it feels good to be with a friend. Mainly any socialising I do is with Harry and that usually involves Tom and Karen as well. I think I've forgotten what it's like to be out on my own and despite it feeling a little surreal, it also feels exciting.

We make our way through the crowd to the bar and I shout, "A white wine please and...?"

I look at Isabel and she nods. "Make that two."

The noise levels are loud in here, so we decide to take our drinks outside to the small courtyard at the rear of the bar. I notice the average age here isn't much younger than mine and relax a little.

We sit in a corner near a wall and Isabel raises her glass. "Cheers, Tina. Thanks for asking me."

I clink her glass with mine and settle down for a gossip.

For most of the evening, we chat about the school, the other parents and life in general. Safe issues that require no deep discussion. Nothing to cause offence, just polite conversation between acquaintances. The trouble is, one drink turns to two, then three and with that comes a looser tongue, so when she looks at me with sympathy and says, "Is everything ok, Tina? I mean, you seem quite sad."

I look up sharply and she flushes. "I'm sorry. Please don't answer that, it's none of my business."

Leaning back in my chair, I sigh heavily as the tears well up in my eyes. "It's fine. To be honest, things are a little shaky at home at the moment."

She looks concerned and I smile ruefully. "The trouble is, I'm desperate to have another baby and the doctors have told me I can't."

Her hand flies to her mouth, and she looks at me with horror. "I'm so sorry, is there any chance they could be wrong?"

"I don't think so. I've been through every possible solution but I'm just not producing any eggs. There's no operation in the world that can magic those necessary ingredients up, so we're at a bit of a loss."

She reaches for my hand and squeezes it with compassion. "I'm sorry, it must be hard."

Nodding, I take another sip of wine and say gloomily, "It's causing so many problems between me and Harry. He told me I had to accept it and look at other ways of having children."

She looks confused. "Like what?"

"Adoption mainly. We aren't married though, never saw the need and that may count against us."

Isabel looks thoughtful. "I'm sure that's not the case anymore. Have you looked into it?"

I smile thinly. "Not really. I suppose I was still hoping for a miracle."

She smiles sweetly. "Well, if there's anything I can do to help, you know, research anything for you or stuff like that just ask. I have quite a lot of time on my hands and could use something to distract me from the usual soap operas I've taken to watching."

I look at her in surprise. "You would really do that… for me?"

She nods. "Of course, after all, what are friends for?"

Suddenly, Isabel looks like an Angel sitting before me. She hasn't judged and offered trite words of support. She's just offered friendship and a practical offer that may help.

I smile gratefully. "Thank you. I really mean that. It's good to have someone to talk to about this. Harry doesn't want to and Karen's so wrapped up in her own problems, I don't want to burden her with mine."

Isabel looks at me sharply, "Karen's having problems. What do you mean?"

I say sadly, "Between me and you, things weren't always so rosy between her and Tom. For a while back there, I thought they were going to split up."

She leans forward. "I'm sorry to hear that. It's nothing I did, is it?"

Laughing, I take another gulp of wine and say in a whisper, "No, it was before you arrived. Tom was always away on business and Karen was left on her own – a lot. They used to argue, and she told me they weren't even having sex anymore."

She looks shocked and I nod. "I know, terrible isn't it? Well, he was quite a workaholic and never had time for her or Jack. I think it got to the point where she was going to ask him for a divorce."

Isabel gasps, "That's terrible. What changed, I mean, they are such a loving couple now, I sure wish I knew their secret?"

"Well, it changed the night Tom was mugged. He took quite a beating and it must have knocked some sense into him because after the shock wore off, he discovered he actually loved his wife and son and has done everything he can to make it up to them. It's quite a fairy story, isn't it?"

She smiles and I don't miss the interest in her eyes. Maybe I shouldn't have told her anything but for some reason, Isabel is proving to be a good listener and I feel as if I can tell her anything.

The wine starts to take effect and I feel my eyes closing and she laughs softly, "Maybe I should get you home."

Giggling, I stand up and swaying slightly, say gratefully, "It's fine, I can walk, it's not far."

Shaking her head, she grasps my hand firmly and pulls me after her. "No, you need a coffee at least and then I'm calling you a cab. My flat's just around the corner, you can sober up a little there before I send you home."

Feeling like a giggling schoolgirl, I grin and say jokingly, "Yes, miss."

Rolling her eyes, Isabel laughs and then pulls me purposefully from the bar.

13

Giggling like schoolgirls, we pile into Isabel's flat and I look around me with surprise. As flat's go, it's quite big but there is hardly anything in here. Just one settee and a small table. No pictures, treasured possessions or anything that usually makes a place home.

Isabel looks a little embarrassed and says sadly, "Not much of a home is it?"

Trying to curb my surprise, I smile. "It's lovely. I like a place with less clutter, it clears the mind."

She smiles but I can tell she doesn't believe me. "Anyway, let's make some coffee and sober up a little. I'm pretty sure Harry won't thank me for leading his wife astray on a rare night out without him."

Thinking about Harry, the alarm bells start ringing and I rummage in my bag for my phone. "Oh no, he'll be worried. I forgot to tell him I was going for a drink."

Isabel looks horrified and I grin sheepishly as I quickly type a text. I'm not prepared to hear his disapproving voice just yet. I'll save that particular pleasure for when I get home.

Sorry babe, I forgot to say I met Isabel, and we went for a drink after class. Just having a coffee won't be long. Is everything ok? Xx

Almost immediately he texts back.

Oh, thanks for the late message. I've been frantic and you could have thought to tell me. Yes, Jamie's fine, thanks for remembering you have a son.

I check my phone again and see he called me at least 20 times and feel bad.

Isabel hands me a coffee and says with concern, "Is everything ok?"

Plastering a smile on my face, I say lightly, "Yes, no problem, although perhaps I should have this and go. I think I may have stayed out a little too long, and it is a school night after all. You'll be shattered tomorrow."

Isabel smiles softly and I stare at her in surprise. She looks so pretty in this light and I never noticed it before. There is an innocence to her, and she's the sort of person you could tell all your secrets to and know they were in safe hands.

She smiles sweetly. "Thank you."

"For what?"

"For being a friend. I don't have many and I want you to know I enjoyed your company."

For some reason, my eyes fill with tears and she looks concerned. "Hey, I didn't mean to make you cry."

Shaking my head, I sit on her couch and sniff. "I'm sorry, it's me. I'm super-emotional at the moment and any kind word or gesture seems to set me off."

She comes and sits beside me and then does a strange thing. She takes the mug from my hand and pulls me by her side, rubbing my shoulder comfortingly. I lay my head against her and we just sit for a moment, side by side in silence as the clock ticks loudly nearby.

After a while, she says softly, "I know a thing or two about being lonely, Tina. It's not a nice feeling, is it?"

I say in a whisper, "No, it isn't."

She carries on rubbing and I like it. It feels so comforting, like a mother comforting her child, taking all the worry away and promising that everything will be ok.

After a while, she says firmly. "I'll call you a cab. You're right, it's late and you should probably be going home."

She jumps up and I immediately wish she hadn't. As she makes the call, I study her. She is calm and in control and has a softness to her that I wish I had myself. I'm pretty sure teaching is the perfect profession for Isabel because she exudes authority and yet is someone you feel could make everything ok.

She finishes the call and I say impulsively, "You know, I really enjoyed this evening. Would you like to do it again sometime?"

Her eyes light up. "I'd like that, thanks."

"What about Saturday night? If Harry can't babysit, you could come over to mine. I'll ask Karen too and we can make a girly night of it."

Isabel's eyes sparkle and I can tell the invitation means a lot.

"Thank you, I'd like that."

As the doorbell rings, I grab my bag and smile. "Great, I'll text you the details. Thanks for the coffee."

She walks with me to the cab and just before I get in, she kisses me lightly on the cheek. "Thanks, Tina. You don't know how much this means to me."

I smile as I get into the cab, pleased that I saw her tonight. I think she will become a good friend and quite frankly I need as many of those as I can get.

Harry is waiting when I get home and I don't miss the anger in his eyes.

As soon as I get inside the door, he rounds on me angrily.

"So, you're back then."

I shrug and say sarcastically. "No prizes for observation darling."

He narrows his eyes and hisses. "You could have called. I thought you were doing a gym class, not drinking with your new best friend until the early hours."

I turn away and he pulls me back angrily. "Don't you ignore me."

I push him hard and say in a dull voice. "So, you want to touch me now. It will be the first time in weeks. Do you want to know why I stayed out so long? Well, it's because I didn't want to come home. This place is sucking all the life out of me because of you."

His eyes flash. "Me?"

"Yes, you. You make me feel anxious, Harry. I can't appear to say or do anything right and you look at me as if I disgust you. The fact you sleep in the spare room most nights tells us something is very wrong with our relationship. Is it because I'm no longer a woman in your eyes? Is the fact I can no longer have children turning you off because I wouldn't blame you?"

A huge sob works its way from deep inside and I turn away before he can see the devastation in my eyes.

However, he pulls me back and I gasp as I see the pain in his. He says gruffly, "I don't know what to do any more, Tina. I'm trying to give you space but it's just driving a wedge between us. I can see you're broken but I don't know how to fix this – you."

The tears splash onto my cheeks like a welcome rain shower after a very hot day. The look in his eyes shows me he is as broken as I am and I sob, "I don't want space from you, I need us to be closer than ever. I need you to love me enough for the both of us because I don't love myself at the moment. I can't deal with this and it's tearing me apart."

He pulls me hard against him and buries his face in my shoulder. No words are spoken just something I need more than oxygen at the moment. The man I love in my arms reassuring me that everything will be alright – *we* will be alright because I wasn't lying, I can't do this on my own.

Tonight, I don't sleep on my own. Tonight, my partner makes love to me like I've wished he would for what feels like forever. In doing so, he chases a few of the demons away and I dare to think that everything may be ok. We have a family already and I'm just being greedy wanting more. I can't risk losing the one I do have but I will need help to get through. I can't lose Harry; it would destroy me.

Long after Harry falls into a deep sleep, I lay in his arms. I watch him and remember the relief I felt when we made love this evening. That closeness, that bond we always thought would make us invincible, frayed a little these last few months. However, now I feel we have made a start on repairing it, and I vow to give up on this whole baby issue and just be thankful for what I already have. As I watch the man I love sleep by my side, at this moment, I have everything.

14

Things seem a little better at home. Maybe my night out helped to clear the air because Harry's been a lot more attentive and I've tried my hardest to get things back to normal.

By the time Saturday comes, I'm feeling much better and text Isabel and Karen to come over to allow Harry a night out with Tom.

I make sure I dress up though and take considerable care in making us some nice food to nibble on and stock up on Prosecco.

Briefly, I wonder if Karen will feel uncomfortable around Isabel but I can't dwell on that. She needs friends and proved a good one to me when I needed it, so it's the least I can do. I'm not sure why but I'm looking forward to seeing Isabel the most. Maybe it's because she's a calming presence in turbulent waters which is why I'm drawn to her.

The doorbell rings interrupting my thoughts and as I answer I see Karen standing behind an excited Jack and she raises her eyes.

"Someone's been looking forward to this evening all day."

Jack says quickly, "Where's Jamie?"

As if on cue, Jamie bounds down the stairs two at a time and Jack says loudly, "I've got Extreme Action, Jamie. Do you want to play?"

Jamie grins. "Cool. Come upstairs, I've got it set up already."

As we watch them go, Karen laughs. "I could do with some extreme action myself."

Giggling, I head towards the kitchen and reach for the Prosecco. "Maybe if you have enough of this, the extreme action may be on the menu later."

"Here's hoping."

As we sip our drinks, I say with interest. "So how, are things with Tom lately? You both seem a different couple from what you were a few months ago. What's your secret?"

Karen smiles mysteriously. "Sex. Lots and lots of lovely toe-curling, basic, dirty sex and then the rest follows."

I almost spit out my drink.

"You lucky bitch, how have you gone from tired Tom to sex beast Tom? Tell me at once so I can use it on Harry."
She shakes her head and looks thoughtful. "You know, it's since he was mugged. It took a good few months before he would even touch me again, although that wasn't unusual. As you know, we were walking a fine line before that night. He was away a lot and always tired and irritable when he

was home. However, I think the mugging made him see things differently. Now family comes first, whereas before he never even appeared to want one."

I nod sympathetically. I remember the endless evenings spent dissecting their marriage. I was shocked to learn that Tom had never wanted children. Jack was a lovely surprise, to him, anyway. Karen always thought it was her pregnancy that glued them together because Tom was so angry with her when she fell pregnant. However, he was also a man who watched the pennies and the thought of handing half of everything he earned over to her was obviously a less attractive option than staying and going through the motions.

Karen soon found out it was the worse thing she could have done because Tom wouldn't touch her after that. The only time they had sex was when Tom decided it was ok. Looking at her now, it's as if that happened to somebody else because I have never seen her looking so radiant.
The doorbell rings and she looks up in surprise. "Are you expecting anyone else?"

Feeling slightly guilty, I say apologetically. "Yes, Isabel."

I don't miss the worry flare in her eyes and feel bad as she says, "Oh, I didn't know you were that friendly."
As I head to answer the door, I say quickly, "We weren't until the other night. I'll fill you in later."

When I open the door and see Isabel standing there, something stirs within me. She looks so pretty, soft and shy and maybe it's the mothering instinct in me but I want to wrap her in cotton wool and protect her.

She smiles sweetly as I step forward and kiss her on the cheek. "Hi, Isabel, you look lovely. What's that scent you're wearing, it's amazing?"

She laughs softly, "It's one of those you make yourself. I went to a store with Eddie and we had it made."

A shadow passes across her face and she says in a small voice, "We were always doing things like that. You know, little days out that had meaning and made memories to cherish."

Feeling bad for her, I pull her close and hug her gently, "I'm sorry. It must be so hard."

She nods. "Yes, but evenings like this help, so thanks for inviting me."

Grinning, I pull her inside. "Think nothing of it, Karen's through here and has a glass of Prosecco with your name on it."

Karen looks up as we enter the room and smiles brightly. "Hi, how are you?"

Isabel smiles and sits beside her on the barstool at the kitchen counter.

"Fine thank you, Karen. I hope you don't mind me crashing your party."

Shaking her head, Karen pushes a drink towards her. "It's not my party, it's Tina's and you're more than welcome. It should be fun."

My heart settles a little as I see they appear comfortable with each other and I say brightly, "Ok, let me feed those two hungry gamers upstairs and then we can get down to the serious business of having a good time."

As the evening wears on, I discover just how much fun Isabel really is. After her earlier shyness, the Prosecco does its job and brings her out of her shell. She has Karen and me in fits of laughter with stories of life as a teacher and I suppose as evenings go, this one could be classed as a success. I do a good job of putting my problems behind me until Isabel says innocently, "Hey, did you know that Marsha Bennett's expecting twins?"

It's like a hammer to my heart and I reach for the glass beside me and take a long gulp, before saying brightly, "No, I didn't."

Karen looks at me with concern and says softly, "That's nice. Oh, Tina, did you see that Take That are in concert next month, do you fancy going?"

She smiles at Isabel. "Do you like Take That, I could get us all tickets if you're up for it?"

Shaking her head, Isabel says gratefully, "I'm not a fan, to be honest. I like classical music and opera but thanks for asking."

She looks at me with interest. "Do you like opera Tina? If you do, I have some amazing DVDs I could lend you."

Maybe it's because the only thing I can think of is Marsha Bennett and her babies, it doesn't strike me as odd that she snubbed Karen so quickly. I don't even register that Karen seems a little put out as I say sadly, "I wish I was Marsha Bennett."

Karen laughs, "Well, I don't. Two babies will be hard work. Think of it, Tina. It may seem like the dream but I'm guessing it's one dressed up in a nightmare."

I'm not sure why, but the tears start to fall and I say emotionally, "It's a dream to me."

In a flash, Isabel is beside me, taking my hand and squeezing it reassuringly. "I'm so sorry, Tina. I didn't mean to upset you."

Karen says tightly, "Tina's quite vulnerable at the moment, especially on this subject."

I say through my tears. "I'm sorry guys. I didn't mean to ruin the evening and maybe it's the alcohol but it doesn't take much to set me off these days."

Isabel strokes my back and says soothingly, "You know, it doesn't have to be this way."

Karen shakes her head and throws her a hard look. "Isabel, it *is* this way for Tina. She has to learn to accept this and move on."

A hint of steel creeps into Isabel's voice and she shakes her head. "I disagree, Karen. You see, there are many options available to Tina and Harry. I think you're forgetting we have more choices than ever now and the fact that Tina isn't able to produce eggs doesn't necessarily mean she won't be a mother again."

There's stunned silence and I look at her in shock. "What do you mean?"

Turning to face me, she takes my hands and looks at me with such a kind look it takes my breath away and then her words knock me for six, "I can give you a baby, Tina. I'll be your surrogate."

15

Karen gasps and I feel the room spinning around me. Isabel's hand is still in mine anchoring me to normality as I whisper, "What did you say?"

She smiles through her tears. "I'll be your surrogate. Ever since I offered to research the subject for you, I can't stop thinking about it. I've done some digging and these days it's easy to arrange. We can have a contract drawn up and keep everything legal and above board and all I'll be is an incubator. I donate my eggs and Harry's sperm fertilises them. But it will be your baby, Tina, yours and Harry's. Surely that's better than using a total stranger or adoption."

I can't believe what I'm hearing and prepare to grab the lifeline like a mountaineer about to fall on the rocks below. Karen interrupts and says in a hard voice, "Stop and think about this properly, both of you."

Isabel shrugs. "Well, I already have. It's the best thing all round. Tina will make a fantastic mum, hell, she already is one and Harry's a good father. It's unlikely I'm about to have my own children anytime soon, so I want to do something nice for two amazing people."

"Nice!"

Karen jumps up and says angrily. "I can't believe you're even putting this out there. This isn't like offering to help someone babysit or clean their home. It's a bit more than 'nice', it's life changing and I'm not sure you've thought this through properly."

As I note the heat in her voice, I rise to Isabel's defence. "Stop it, Karen. Don't be so mean to Isabel. I actually think this is the most amazing offer I've ever had. She is so generous and kind and I don't deserve it."

Isabel says softly, "You deserve this more than anyone I've ever met. Please say you'll think about it because I've thought of nothing else since the other night."

"The other night?"

We look at Karen who is staring at us both with an expression of pure disbelief. I almost want to giggle at the fact she looks so disapproving and squeeze Isabel's hand, saying lightly, "Yes, the other night Isabel and I had a bit too much to drink after the gym. I kind of unburdened myself to her and well, you know how emotional I get."

Karen looks at us with a mixture of anger and worry. "Please think this through. Sleep on it and don't make any rash decisions. This is serious and will affect so many lives. Don't enter into anything on a whim."

The door slams and we look up as Harry and Tom enter the room. Harry beams, "Have you had fun, girls?"

There's an awkward silence and Karen says in a hard voice, "You could call it that."

Tom looks at her in surprise as she jumps up. "I think we should go. Tom could you call Jack, it's getting late and we should leave Tina and Harry to get some sleep?"

Turning to me, she says urgently. "Think about what I said. We'll talk about this tomorrow."

Isabel has grown quiet and I feel a little bad. It's obvious that Karen's angry with her and I don't know why. I mean, this is such an amazing offer and if anything, she should be thanking Isabel. However, Karen doesn't like her, it's obvious to me and I wonder if it's because of Tom. I didn't miss the way that Isabel's eyes went straight to him as they walked through the door. She *devoured* him with her eyes and I wonder if Karen noticed.

Tom only had eyes for his wife though which is unusual in itself. A few months ago, Tom would have ignored Karen in a room full of strangers. Now she is his first thought, and it gives me hope for Harry and I.

I know Harry used to look at me like that once and I'm pretty sure, with Isabel's help, he will again because I already know my answer. I will jump at the chance for this baby and I just need to convince

Harry to stand with me every step of the way because this is suddenly the most important thing in my life and Isabel is the one who can make it happen. If Karen doesn't like it, she will have to deal with it because my minds made up already. I will take her offer with both hands and nothing will get in my way.

As soon as Karen and Tom leave, Harry looks at me sharply. "Is everything ok?"

Isabel looks a little uncomfortable and I nod, patting the seat beside me. "More than ok, darling. I think you should sit down and listen to what Isabel has suggested."

He looks a little confused and Isabel smiles at me reassuringly. "I meant what I said, Tina. Tell Harry and see what he thinks."

He says firmly, "Will somebody please tell me what's going on because its obvious something is."

Taking a deep breath, I say happily, "Isabel has made us the most fantastic offer, darling. She knows we are having difficulties having another child and has been researching ways we can."

He looks at her in disbelief. "What ways?"

She smiles softly. "This may seem a little strange, Harry but I have offered to be a surrogate for your new baby."

He shakes his head. "What are you talking about?"

Smiling at Isabel, I take his hand and say with excitement, "Isabel has offered to have a baby for us. Isn't that amazing?"

"What?"

Harry's voice is loud and laced with shock and disbelief. I feel a little bad about hitting him with this so forcefully but I need to start this process before Isabel has second thoughts. I know it's selfish but my need is overwhelming my conscience at the moment.

Isabel looks a little uncomfortable. "Maybe I should go and leave you both to discuss this in private. It's a lot to think about. Can I use your phone to call a cab, I appear to be out of charge on mine?"

Harry appears to be in shock and I feel bad and turn to him and smile. "Listen, honey. I know this is a shock. Maybe you should drop Isabel home and she can fill you in on the way. Obviously, we won't go ahead if you're against it but please hear her out at least."

Isabel looks worried. "It's ok, I can get a cab. I'm sure Harry needs to get his breath back after we knocked it out of him."

He shakes his head slowly and as if on autopilot says, "No, Tina's right, I'll drop you home. I haven't had a drink tonight, so you'll be perfectly safe."

Then he says in a firmer voice. "Listen, whatever you've been discussing, you need to stop and think. I'm not sure how these things work but I'm guessing things aren't as straight forward as you believe."

He turns to me and says firmly. "I'm meaning you the most in this, babe. I know you'll do anything for a baby but I'm not sure this is the best option. Don't go running away with this idea now that it's planted in your mind. This is serious and I'm not going to let you drag us into something that will destroy us."

Feeling a little angry, I stare at him with a hard look. "I hear you but you need to think about this with a clear head. Talk it through with Isabel and think about it carefully. All I ask is that you *do* think about it and not just reject it out of hand. This could be an amazing future for us, honey if you just look at it objectively."

Shaking his head, Harry jumps up and says curtly, "Are you ready?"

As Isabel makes to follow him, I pull her back and hug her tightly, whispering, "Thank you."

Just for a moment, she hugs me back, and it feels so good knowing she's with me on this. I can't explain it but I know this is going to happen. I know that Isabel was sent to us for this reason and despite the circumstances that brought her here, this was the reason they did.

As she pulls away, she looks at me with determination and whispers, "Everything will be ok, I promise you that."

As I watch her follow Harry, something tells me it will be. Don't ask me how I know, maybe it's a sixth sense but tonight my path in life shifted and suddenly, the future looks a lot brighter.

16

"No, and that's my final word on the matter!"

I can't believe what I'm hearing. Harry is standing there with his arms crossed and I know that look. He is determined and this will be a difficult few days if not weeks until I can convince him to come around to my way of thinking.

I try a different tack. Staring at him with defeat, I say in a small voice, "Ok."

As I turn away, he reaches out and places his hand on my shoulder and spins me around to face him. "Is that it, ok?"

I shrug miserably. "What do you want me to say? I mean, I've made it pretty clear how much I want this over the last few days. Surely you can tell how much this means to me and yes, I know I'm asking too much of you and Isabel. Maybe you're right and this is all pie in the sky but I suppose I'm a believer in fate and miracles, so it will take me a while to come to terms with your decision."

Harry pulls me to him and says softly, "You know it's for the best, don't you?"

I say nothing and just squeeze my eyes tightly shut. I can't give up now when I'm so close and if I know Harry he'll soon come around to my way of thinking.

As I start the usual cleaning routine, I try to push away the anxiety. What if Harry doesn't agree – ever? I'm not sure I could deal with this after having been so close. Isabel has been amazing through it all and explained to Harry what it involves. When he dropped her home, he didn't come home for several hours. When he did, he explained they had talked long into the night and she told him what was involved. Then he drove around to think it through but needed more time to do his own research. Over the next few days, he looked into it and Isabel came over and we discussed it further. However, today he gave me his final decision, and it wasn't the one I wanted to hear.

My thoughts are interrupted by a gentle tug on my jumper. "Mum, can I go and pay at Jack's?"

"What? Oh, yes, that's nice, whatever..."

As Jamie races towards the door, I say sharply, "Wait."

He looks around in surprise and I grab my bag. "I'll come with you. I could do with talking to Karen."

I feel a little bad because, after that evening, I've been a little cold with her. I didn't like her reaction to Isabel's kind offer and when she came around the next day, she was quite vocal in her disapproval.

Subsequently, I was quite short with her and I feel bad. After all, she was just looking out for me and I should be more understanding and appreciative.

She answers the door and looks at me warily as I smile nervously. Jamie races past me and up the stairs to Jack's room and Karen smiles weakly. "I'm sorry, Tina."

The relief is enormous. "No, I'm sorry Karen. I should never have got angry with you. You were just looking out for me and I apologise."

She opens her arms and I walk into them gladly, sniffing, "I've missed you."

Pulling back, she rolls her eyes. "We're a right couple of idiots, aren't we? Come in and I'll put the kettle on."

As I follow her into the kitchen, everything falls back into place. The friendship we always took for granted faced a challenge we both weren't prepared for and I vow that whatever happens with Isabel, I will never shut Karen out again.

Turning to me, she says thoughtfully, "I've been thinking about your situation – you know, with Isabel."

I feel a little apprehensive as she shakes her head. "I suppose I was so wrapped up in what happened with her and the whole Tom situation, I disregarded what she said. I mean, it was a generous offer and I don't blame you for reaching for it gratefully. I would do the same in your shoes but I was worried."

I nod in agreement. "I understand, I'd probably feel the same if it was you. I don't know though, there's something about Isabel that makes me think it will be ok. I know you had an issue with her regarding Tom but that proved wrong in the end, or so we think, anyway. Even if he did have a thing with her in the past, it's obvious it was meaningless, to him at least. He doesn't look at her in any way other than as an acquaintance and you have absolutely nothing to worry about."

Karen nods. "The trouble is, there's this part of me that doesn't trust her. She had Tom's watch for god's sake. How did she have it unless he left it there? It's too much of a coincidence and to be honest, it's driving me mad. I can't bring it up again because he can't deal with any reminders of what happened. What would you do in my situation?"

I shrug. "The same as you, I suppose. What if it *was* Tom and they came clean? Would it change what you have together now? I mean, would you give up your new found happiness to punish him for straying before? It's obvious he's changed and a million times for the better. Sometimes I think we should just let things go and move on."

Karen nods and pushes a mug of tea across the counter before taking the seat beside me.

"So, tell me about her offer. What's the latest?"

Sighing, I stare into the mug as if the answer lurks there. "Harry said no."

She shakes her head and says sadly "I thought he might."

"Why?"

"Because men find these things hard to deal with. He is probably worried about all the things you haven't even considered yet?"

"Such as?"

She sighs. "Such as the emotional attachment. For example, Isabel may well be doing this to help you out but what if she bonds with her baby and then won't let it go? Harry would be a father to another woman's child and it would be a mess."

I stare at her with a hard look. "She wouldn't be able to, we would sign a contract."

"I'm not so sure, Tina. The law may be one thing but asking a woman to give up her child to another is a law of nature that no jury would rule against."

I feel angry and a little alarmed at her words. "She wouldn't."

Karen shrugs. "She might. Also, what about Jamie? He may find this hard to understand. It's a little weird for him, his teacher having his baby brother or sister. How do you think he will react?"

I don't really know how to answer her which reminds me how little I've thought of him in all of this. "He will love to have a sibling. I'm sure that once he's got over the shock, he'll love the idea."

Karen shakes her head. "Maybe if he was younger, but Jamie is 6 going on 7. It will just be annoying for him. He won't be able to play with the baby; they won't grow up together and he may resent him or her."

Her voice softens, and she reaches for my hand.

"Listen, I know how much this means to you but maybe Harry's right. There's a lot to think about and although it was a kind offer, I don't think you know enough about Isabel to fully trust her with your life like this. Give it time and if after a few months you're still convinced it's a good thing, then maybe look into it again."

I smile sadly and nod, although I know there's a huge part of me that just won't give this up. I don't know what it is, maybe a force of nature, a mother's instincts, I don't know but I can't get this out of my head. I have a chance of bringing another life into this world, albeit through a very different way. Surely that's a small sacrifice in making my family complete.

17

Over the next few weeks, I do everything possible to bring some normality back into my life. I know I'm withdrawn and cold towards Harry but I can't shift the huge ball of resentment I'm feeling towards him because he won't agree to what I know is in our best interests.

Subsequently, he goes out more and so do I – apart. He heads out to the pub or to the gym and I have started going to the classes at the gym regularly with Isabel. Sometimes Karen comes too but I can tell she feels uncomfortable around Isabel. Isabel is always friendly no matter what, and I feel irritated by Karen. I mean, it looks as if Tom did stray with Isabel and if anyone has any right to feel angry about it, it's her. However, she is always sweet and kind and only treats Karen with genuine friendliness and respect.

Despite what I always thought, I find myself drifting away from Karen a little, which only pushes me closer to Isabel as a result.

So, I'm pleased when Harry tells me he wants to go on a camping trip with Jamie at the weekend which will free me up to organise something nice with Isabel. He looks surprised when I say happily, "That sounds an amazing idea. Jamie will love it."

He looks a little concerned. "Are you sure? I mean, I don't like leaving you on your own for two days."

"It's fine, I'll call the girls and see if they fancy catching a movie or a pizza. It will be nice to have some 'me' time."

Looking a little concerned, he says softly, "Are you sure it's a good idea to invite Isabel? Maybe you should spend it with Karen. I've noticed you don't seem as close as you used to be."

I push away the spark of irritation that flares inside and say angrily, "You mean you don't like the idea of me spending cosy evenings with Isabel because you're afraid she'll bring up the pregnancy again."

Sighing, he runs his fingers through his hair and looks worried.

"Maybe I am, it's just I thought things were getting back to normal and I don't want anything to stir it all up again. You're doing so well and I don't want this to set you back."

I put my hands on my hips and stare at him with a hard expression. "Things haven't been normal around here for months, Harry. If you think this life we're living is, then you're very much mistaken."

He looks surprised. "What are you talking about?"

"The fact you walk on eggshells around me half the time. The fact you walk out of a room when an advert for babies or children comes on. Because you still can't bear to touch me and we're living more like flatmates than partners. The fact you spend most evenings out with your friends rather than home with your family and because I feel as if I have lost my best friend as well as my partner and need all the kindness I can get at the moment."

He makes towards me as Jamie flies into the room. "Dad, I've reached level 15. Can I show you?"

Harry says distractedly, "Of course, I'll be right there."

Grabbing a packet of crisps from the cupboard, Jamie races back upstairs before I even have time to yell at him for spoiling his tea and Harry says sadly, "I think we need to talk, don't you?"

I'm not sure why but something in his voice rings the alarm bells and causes my heart to beat frantically inside me. There's a look in his eyes I've never seen before and it makes me stop and think for a moment. "Dad, hurry up."

I nod towards the stairs. "Go and see to Jamie first. Maybe you're right, maybe we do need to talk but not now. Let's think about it over the weekend and talk when you get back because I don't want anything to spoil your time with Jamie. I'll be fine and maybe a break of sorts is just what we need. You go, I'll be fine with my friends."

"Daaaad!!!"

Harry smiles ruefully as he shouts, "Coming!"

As he heads upstairs, I lean on the counter for support. What just happened? I saw it in his eyes. Harry is struggling in his own way, just as much and I'm such a bitch I haven't thought past my own needs how this is affecting him. Maybe I should consider him a little more and make it up to him when he gets back.

The weekend arrives and as I wave off my family, I feel strangely excited for the next couple of days. It's been so tense in the house, I'm quite glad to see the car disappearing around the corner and as I close the door, I relish the silence of an empty house. Perfect.

For the next few hours, I clean everything, confident that it will remain tidy for the next two days. Once I've finished, I look around me with satisfaction. A tidy home always helps things appear easier, and I feel invigorated and ready to take on the world.

I've arranged to go out with Isabel tonight. We're going to watch the latest chick flick that nobody would go with me to see. Karen and Tom are away visiting her family which actually made me feel more relieved than it should. At least I wouldn't be feeling awkward around the two of them. They try to get along but there's always an atmosphere between them that's hard to ignore.

I suppose because I have lots of it, I take a long time getting ready. I take care with my appearance and decide to wear a smart dress that hasn't had an occasion to go to for quite a while.

Isabel said she would drive, so I have time to relax before she arrives and put my feet up with a chilled glass of white wine while I wait.

Bang on 6.30 she rings the doorbell and as I open the door, I smile with appreciation. "You look amazing, Isabel. I love that colour on you."

I'm not lying as she stands there blushing, looking pretty in pink. Her hair is brushed and gleaming and her makeup done to accentuate her pretty face. She is also wearing a nice dress that clings to her curves in all the right places and I wonder how on earth she hasn't been snapped up already by a very lucky guy?

She smiles shyly. "You look beautiful, Tina. Maybe we should head straight out, I think the traffic's bad and if we want to eat first, we need to get going."

Once I've locked the house, I follow her to the car, and we set off for a fun filled relaxed evening. This is something I need more than food at the moment because tonight I need to unwind as a matter of urgency.

Over dinner, we talk about things that any friend would. Gossip about people we know, hair, makeup, books, films, you name it, we speak about it and discover we share most of the same interests.

I make sure to pay and Isabel shakes her head. "No, let me, you can't pay for me, it's not right."

I say fairly sternly, "Nonsense. It's the least I can do after what you offered to do for me."

She looks a little surprised. "Oh, have you thought any more about that – the offer, I mean."

Maybe it's the wine I drank giving me false hope but I smile brightly and nod. "I think Harry's coming around to the idea. He's not there yet but we're going to have another chat when he gets back from the trip. I know I'm going to do my utmost to persuade him and may even roll out the naughty underwear. That usually makes him agree to anything."

Isabel blushes and I laugh. "What, haven't you ever used sex to get what you want?"

She looks horrified and then giggles adorably. "Unlike you, I've never had to. Unfortunately, my relationships have been short and sweet and I've never needed to persuade my boyfriends to do anything."

She looks so despondent I feel bad for her and say gently, "You know, one day you'll meet the man of your dreams."

She nods and says quietly, "The trouble is, I thought I already had. You see, it's the not knowing that I can't deal with. The police never found Eddie's body and everything about the situation is mysterious. He lived alone in what almost appeared temporary accommodation. He never introduced me to his family or friends and never shared any details of his life with me. I've come to the conclusion that I was just a dirty little secret he wanted to keep to himself."

I watch as a hard look flashes in her eyes and she says bitterly, "The trouble with secrets is they have a habit of getting out. One day this will come out and I'll be able to move on. Until then I'm in limbo and don't feel as if I can move on until it's resolved."

She looks up and her face relaxes. "Anyway, you don't want to hear my sob story. The whole purpose of this weekend is to cheer you up, so come on, girlfriend, let's go and indulge in some eye candy of the sweetest kind and pretend there's a Prince Charming out there for us all."

She takes my hand and pulls me from the restaurant and it feels nice. Two friends together with no cares or worries, for tonight anyway.

Looking back, I should have frozen time then because that's where it all began to go downhill. After that night, my life was set to self-destruct and there was nothing I could do about it.

18

It's been ages since I enjoyed a film as much. Maybe it's because it's not the usual boy's film I end up accompanying Jamie to, or Harry for that matter. He usually likes films on war or total devastation. Or it could be the company? Isabel and I share a tub of popcorn and it feels good. We laugh at the same lines in the movie and giggle as our fingers collide as we dive in for the same piece of popcorn. I feel relaxed around her. She's proving to be one big surprise in my life and I can't remember a time without her in it. Life is uncomplicated around her. She makes everything seem better and has an easy personality that draws me out of myself.

Once the film finishes, we head outside and not wanting the evening to end, I say brightly, "Shall we grab a drink somewhere?"

She shakes her head and says regretfully, "I'm a little tired. Maybe because the lights were so dim in the cinema, it's made me feel quite sleepy, actually."

Rolling my eyes, I laugh. "You're a lightweight. How old are you?"

She grins. "24."

I look at her in surprise. "Goodness, a whole 10 years younger than me. I feel so old."

She smiles sweetly. "You don't look ten years older than me. I hope I look as amazing as you when I'm your age."

"I'm sure you'll look a lot better than me. Anyway, do you fancy a coffee at mine to wake you up?"

"Thanks, that sounds amazing."

As we head back, I think about Isabel. 24 is an age where you have the world at your feet. She's good looking, funny, clever and a nice person. The trouble is, she's been unlucky it seems and hasn't been able to find that relationship yet that she deserves.

As soon as we get inside, I kick off my shoes and smile. "Come in and make yourself at home. I'll put the kettle on."

She flops down on the sofa and groans. "This feels so nice; I can't believe how much I ache."

Laughing, I head over and say sternly, "Here, lean forward and I'll give you a neck massage. I'm quite good at them, apparently."

She shifts around and I sit beside her and start massaging her shoulders. She groans and says gratefully, "You're right you're good at this. That feels amazing."

I say sternly, "Shh, silence please, so you get the full effect."

As I work away, the silence surrounds us with only the sound of the passing cars outside to spoil the moment. As I work on Isabel's shoulders, I find myself relaxing too. Her skin feels so soft and I can smell that amazing scent she uses.

I start to feel a little warm and wonder if I've had too much to drink because it strikes me how much I'm enjoying feeling her skin beneath my fingers.

She arches back and murmurs, "That feels so good."

I'm not sure why but I have an overwhelming urge to sweep her hair away from her neck and kiss that soft perfumed skin beneath my fingers. Leaning forward, I take a deep breath and surround myself with her scent. She smells good, innocent and like home.

Feeling a little shocked, I pull away and say briskly, "Um... that should do the trick. Now, let me get that coffee."

She settles back on the sofa and says gratefully, "That was amazing, thank you."

Feeling a little wrong-footed, I leave the room and head to the kitchen and when inside I lean my head against the fridge door. What just happened? It was as if I wanted Isabel. I mean, really wanted her. I wanted to feel her lips on mine and her skin against my skin. This is weird, I've never wanted to be with a woman before but I wanted it more than anything then. What's happening to me?

Suddenly, I'm aware I'm not alone and look up to see Isabel standing in the doorway, looking a little worried.

"Are you ok, Tina? Do you feel unwell?"

Shaking away any thoughts I may have for her, I smile. "I'm ok, don't worry, I just felt a little dizzy there for a moment."

She looks concerned. "Maybe I should leave. You could get an early night and take advantage of having the house to yourself."

She turns as if to go and I say sharply, "No, wait."

As she turns towards me, I see the same look in her eyes that I'm sure is in mine and she says in a small voice, "I really think I should go, Tina."

I'm not sure who moves first but suddenly we are standing face to face and I can tell she feels the same. Call it a basic instinct but it's in her eyes.

Reaching out, I stroke the side of her face and notice how her lip trembles as she looks at me with those soft, innocent, eyes and says breathlessly, "I should go but I can't."

There is that moment where you have an opening to escape from the rabbit hole. You peer into it and make a judgement based on what you know is the wrong thing. However, fate drives you down a different path and your heart is the steering wheel. My rabbit hole is opening up right in front of me and I don't even think.

I jump.

Suddenly, my lips find hers and rather than pull away, she presses them tightly against mine. As our tongues meet, I am carried away by the sweetest of senses. I couldn't stop myself if I tried, as I share the forbidden with Isabel and taste destruction. We kiss like two would be lovers and rather than pull away with confusion and apologies, we go with the moment and before I know what's happening, I find my life spiralling out of control on a haze of forbidden lust.

When I wake the next morning, for the first time in weeks, I'm not alone. However, this time the person sharing my bed isn't Harry.

I close my eyes and think back on a life-altering night. I slept with Isabel. Correction, I made love to Isabel. I know it was love because I felt it. Every touch, every kiss, every moan and every feeling were surrounded by love.

As I watch her sleeping peacefully, it strikes me how beautiful she is. Even with no makeup and with her eyes closed, she looks so perfect. Rather than feel ashamed, I feel as if I have found something I was always searching for. I'm not sure why but I feel as if Isabel's my soul mate. We think along the same lines, like the same things and obviously share a desire for one another.

I don't even feel guilty about cheating on Harry. After all, how can something be wrong when it's obviously written in the stars. Yes, this complicates things but now I've found this feeling, I'm holding onto it like a drug addict loathe to come down from a high.

Suddenly, Isabel stirs and I see her eyelids flicker. I watch in wonder as she wakes up and opens her eyes. However, she obviously doesn't share my certainty because she springs from the bed and says in a shocked voice, "Oh my god, what have we done?"

19

Sitting up, I stare at her in confusion.

"What do you mean, you know what happened?"

I don't like the way her eyes fill with terror and she starts grabbing her clothes and struggles into them.

I say in surprise, "Is something the matter?"

She looks at me in horror. "I'm sorry, Tina, I don't want this; it isn't me and shouldn't have happened."

"What do you mean, of course, it should have? If anything was the right thing it was that. Please, Isabel, let's talk about this."

She backs away from me and says in a choked voice.

"I'm sorry, I don't want to talk about it. If anything, I want to forget it ever happened."

Her words wound me more than any sharp knife and I gasp, "Why? Don't you remember, it was magical? *We* were magical together. Last night everything fell into place. My life made sense, and it's because of you, Isabel. You're my future. Think about it, we could go ahead with the surrogacy, with or without Harry. I'm sure we could find a sperm donor or something. Then we could set up home together, with Jamie and the baby – our baby. Yes, I thought about this long into the night. This was always meant to happen. We were destined to be together."

My words spill out in a rush and I have control over them. However, as soon as they leave my lips, I can tell they are not what she wants to hear. It's true, I did lie awake thinking of the perfect life we would have together. The feelings I felt last night shocked me. I have never felt as strongly about anyone as I do her, not even Harry who I've been with for twelve years. In fact, I made up my mind that Harry was no longer what I wanted. My life with Isabel was all I could think of and the way she is looking at me fills me fear.

I say carefully, "Listen, I know it's a shock, totally unexpected and we couldn't have seen this coming but think about it. Please Isabel, at least try to see how good we could be."

She faces me with hurt and anger swirling in her beautiful eyes which makes me want to hold her and reassure her that everything will be ok. She backs away and stutters, "Listen, I'm flattered, really I am but you've got it wrong. I like men, I always have. I've never wanted to be with a woman and last night well, it took me by surprise. Now I'm awake and thinking straight I don't like what we did and just want to forget it ever happened. I'm sorry but that's my decision, please respect it."

She turns to go and I say almost desperately, "Your offer still stands though, doesn't it?"

Slowly, she turns to face me and I see a hint of pity in her eyes. "I'm sorry, no. The offer doesn't stand. I um… think we should maybe stay clear of each other from now on, this was a mistake and I'm sorry but I need to go."

She pulls open the door and I stumble after her.

"Please wait, let's talk about this."

She flies down the stairs and wrenches open the door, racing towards her car without a backward glance. I don't care that all I'm wearing is a thin satin robe with nothing on my feet. I don't care that I stand on my driveway calling out her name in agony and I don't care that I sink to my knees when the car pulls away taking my future with it. I don't care because I am broken. She has broken me and I'm not sure if I'll be the same again.

Somehow, I drag myself inside and sob uncontrollably. I don't even think about Harry or Jamie; all I can think about is that Isabel left. Why can't she see what I can? I told her how good it could be. We could be a family, a team and take on the world together. I was prepared to leave Harry for her and she still couldn't see the sacrifice I was making – for her.

It takes me a while to muster up the energy to get ready and I go through the motions while my head is somewhere else. How can I possibly go on if Isabel isn't in my life?

Then it hits me. She was scared, yes - that was it. Maybe her own feelings scared her and she fled to get a grip. Maybe she's as scared as I am and needs time to think about things. How could I be so stupid, of course, she was scared? I'll give her time to settle down and then go and pay her a visit. I'm sure when she's had time to think about everything, she'll see it's for the best.

Feeling a little brighter, I set about clearing up and preparing a meal for Harry and Jamie. As I cook, I plan out in my head how I'll break the news to Harry that I'm leaving and taking Jamie with me. Maybe he will leave and Isabel can move in. It will be a little strange at first for Jamie but it's not unusual these days.

I'm not sure at what moment my world descended into madness but to me, it all makes perfect sense. Isabel is my future and I won't let it go so easily.

When Harry and Jamie return the house descends into its usual chaos. Jamie rushes in like a whirlwind and merely says a brief, "Hi Mum," before racing to the cupboard and grabbing some crisps before flying back upstairs.

Harry rolls his eyes. "No prizes for guessing where he's heading. All he spoke of was getting some extreme action as soon as he got home."

He moves across and pulls me tightly against him and groans. "I must admit the same thought had crossed my mind."

I feel a prickle of alarm as he holds me tightly. I'm not sure why but this feels wrong. Harry has only been gone for a couple of days but it feels as if he left a long time ago. Laughing nervously, I push him away and say brightly, "Yes, um… well, you must be starving. I'll make you a sandwich."

I don't miss the hurt flare up in his eyes as he notes the rebuff and as I distance myself from him physically, it's not half as far as I am mentally. The thought of being with Harry after what I experienced last night doesn't compare, and it's in this moment, I realise just what happened. I fell out of love with Harry a long time ago because the love I now feel for Isabel, is much deeper than the one I ever felt for him.

Harry is upset, I can tell, as he says in a hurt voice, "I'll just go and unpack then."

Nodding, I say firmly, "Make sure you put all the dirty clothes in the laundry basket and not on the floor like you usually do. I've managed to keep this house clean and tidy for two days and I want it to stay that way for as long as possible."

The door slamming is all the answer I get and I sigh. This is a problem that I'm not sure how to resolve. I need to speak to Isabel to sort things out with her because until I do that, I can't settle things here.

Impulsively I grab my phone and text her.

Hey, I'm sorry about earlier. I don't know what came over me. Maybe we could meet up and talk about it. Say later on today? Xx

I set about making lunch but keep on glancing nervously at the phone, anticipating her reply.

However, she doesn't and by late afternoon I'm frantic. I know the text was delivered but there's been no reply. I know I shouldn't, but I try again.

Hey, I'm not sure if you got my last text but I really need to explain things. Please call or text me to arrange something. Xx

Again, I wait anxiously and try to do anything I can to distract me but it's as if I can't think of anything else. The day turns to dusk and as we settle down to watch the TV, I'm on tenterhooks. She must have received my texts, why isn't she replying?

Harry is also pre-occupied and just sits in his usual chair flicking between programmes. I'm not sure if we speak two words to each other, except idle comments here and there. I don't ask about his trip and he doesn't ask what I've been doing. It's as if there's a cold wall of ice forming between us and I'm not sure if it will ever melt.

It gets to 8 pm and Harry looks at me with a blank expression. "Listen, Tina, I'm not sure what's happening here, but it's obvious we need to talk."

I nod, feeling wretched but not because of the conversation we're about to have, it's because there's still no word from Isabel.

Moving across, he comes and sits beside me and takes my hand in his. Fighting the urge to snatch it away, I look at him irritably.

"What is it, Harry? I need to make sure Jamie's in bed and not playing on that damned game still."

He looks at me sadly and says, "I'm leaving you."

20

I just stare at him blankly. He shakes his head and says sadly, "I'm sorry, Tina. I've tried my best, but this isn't working anymore. It's obvious from your behaviour since I returned. You don't want me and to be brutally honest, I stopped wanting you a long time ago."

He returns to his seat and faces me with a hard expression as I stare at him in shock. Not because he's leaving, actually it's a relief but because he told me he stopped wanting me a long time ago.

He says in a hard voice. "Don't you have anything to say?"

I shake my head. "Not really. It's pretty obvious when you come to think of it. How long have you known though?"

He shrugs. "A while. In fact, I think it was long before you started wanting another baby. I suppose you changed and were no longer the woman I fell in love with. You weren't interested in me and I always thought you had sex with me to keep me happy rather than yourself. When you decided on another baby, I thought it may be just what we needed to bring us closer. The trouble is, it became obvious to me I was just a sperm donor because it became like a military operation. It had to be when you thought you stood the most chance of conceiving and not because you wanted to make love to me. I felt used and quite frankly as if you thought I wasn't up to the job. I could see in your eyes, you blamed me every month that passed, and you still weren't pregnant."

Standing up, I pace the floor and say angrily, "Then why didn't you say anything if it was such a chore? You know, it takes two people to make a relationship work, it's not all down to me."

He says carefully. "I tried; god knows I tried hard. You've changed, Tina. I'm not sure how but it's as if you're obsessed. I can't get through to you and I've stopped wanting to try."

I say tightly, "Is there someone else, is that it? I mean, you spend so much time out with your so-called friends, it must be another woman dragging you away."

He shakes his head sadly. "You see, here you go again, it has to be my fault. You just can't see that for a relationship to work it takes two people who want it to. To be honest, I'm not sure if you ever really did."

"What's that supposed to mean? Of course, I wanted it to work. We have a son for god's sake, why wouldn't I want it to work for his sake."

Harry hisses, "Exactly. You want the perfect family, to the outside world, anyway. You want the nice house, the adoring husband and the 2.5

children. You haven't worked since Jamie was born and now you can, you show no interest in going back. All day you clean and cook and have coffee with your so-called friends. You have nothing in your life to define you and you think that having children will give you purpose. Well, newsflash, children grow up and leave and then where will you be? You need to re-discover Tina Jenkins before you'll ever be happy."

Sinking down on the settee, I put my head in my hands and sob. Harry comes and sits beside me and puts his arm around my shoulders and I shrug it off angrily. The trouble is, I'm not crying for him and not even because of what he's said. I'm crying because during his rant I noticed a text come through on my phone that has destroyed me.

Leave me alone!

Harry says in a soft voice. "I'm sorry, babe. I didn't mean to do this tonight. I wanted to see if we could maybe get counselling and work at things but you rubbed me up the wrong way and I lost my temper. Do you want to talk about it, maybe try to think of a way we can sort this out without falling out?"

Wiping the tears away, I look at him with a stony expression. "No, I don't think I do. Actually, I think you've said it all. I just want you to leave, move out and leave me to sort my life out. I don't want you telling me how much of a failure I am as a partner and a mother. I don't want you 'trying' as you say, when it's obvious we grew apart years ago. I don't want you making me feel inferior and I don't want *you*. So, maybe it's best if we do go our separate ways and just work together to make things right for Jamie. I'm sure he'll be happier if we're happier, so I think it's best if you just go."

Harry nods and moves towards the door. "What will we tell Jamie?"

I shrug. "The truth. We are splitting up and it's not going to affect him. He'll still have two parents who love him and will always be there for him, just not in the same home."

Harry stares at me incredulously. "It's not going to affect him? How can you possibly say that?"

I shrug. "Of course, he'll be upset but he'll get over it. Maybe call him now and we'll do it tonight and then you can leave."

I turn away because I can't bear the look of disgust on Harry's face. My words seem cold even to my ears but it's as if I can't think rationally anymore. I just want to get this over with so I can move on. The most important thing is to repair my relationship with Isabel because now I've had a taste of perfection, I want it forever.

Harry says coldly. "I'll go and talk to Jamie. Let me speak to him first."

I shrug and straighten the cushion on the seat he vacated as he closes the door. Maybe I'm a coward but I can't face telling my son that his father's leaving. Harry has made that decision so he can break the bad news and look like the bad guy in this. Once I've sorted things with Isabel, Jamie will see how amazing life can be when two people love each other. We will make sure he has the best life possible and hopefully, that will involve a brother or sister to make our family complete.

Reaching out, I pick up the phone and study the message. She's angry and upset. Maybe I put too much pressure on her. I'll go and see her at school tomorrow. I'm sure when she sees me it will all fall into place. I know we're meant to be together; I feel it in my broken heart.

21

Last night Harry left. He packed a few things and left without any tears or tantrums from me, anyway. Jamie cried - a lot. When Harry told him, it destroyed them both. I could tell Harry was on the edge of breaking down and I tried to be strong enough for everyone, although inside I was as destroyed as they were. Just not for the same reason.

I sat with Jamie long after Harry left and tried to answer his questions as best I could. He finally fell asleep in the early hours after having used up any tears he had left.

I sat beside him as he slept but my tears fell for a different reason. I couldn't cry for Harry because I know this is the best for everyone. He was right that we had grown apart and now he's gone I feel as if a burden has lifted and I'm free. Jamie is my priority now and so, as the morning breaks, I vow to do what's best for him.

Breakfast is a strange affair. The toast tastes like cardboard in my mouth and Jamie doesn't even touch his cereal. Harry's chair is painfully empty and I can see Jamie staring at it with a lost look in his eyes. My heart goes out to him because Harry is a good father. That won't change but Jamie won't be thinking about that now. The clock ticks on and I say gently, "Do you want to miss school today?"

He shakes his head. "It's ok. I just want to get out of the house, really."

I smile sympathetically and say brightly, "Well, maybe you should get ready then. I'll drop you in, I'll just text Karen and see if she wants me to take Jack as well."

Jamie scoots off to change and I text Karen.

Hey, I have to take Jamie to school this morning and I'll fill you in later. Do you want me to drop Jack as well? Xx

Great, thanks. I'll bring him around. Is everything ok? Xx

Not really, I'll explain later. xx

I pull out all the stops getting ready and make sure I put on my prettiest dress and makeup. I want Isabel to see me as a woman, not a mother and convince her that I'm the one she wants.

The doorbell rings and I answer it, smiling as Jack pushes past me to find Jamie. Karen looks concerned as she follows me inside.

"Is everything ok?"

Shaking my head, I sigh sadly. "Not really. Harry left last night."

"Left!"

"Yes, to be honest, it was a long time coming but Jamie's taking it badly."

Karen moves across and hugs me gently. "Are you ok?"

I feel the tears well up as I hear the kindness in her voice and say sadly, "I will be. Jamie is all I can think of at the moment and I just want his world to be happy again. Harry and I will sort things out but it's still not fair on Jamie."

Karen nods. "It's very sad. Is there no chance of making it work?"

"No, I think that ship sailed a long time ago. It's for the best and now I just need to make a new life without Harry by my side."

The boys run downstairs and I can see that Jack looks upset. Obviously, Jamie told him and I'm glad. He needs a friend right now, someone to confide in and who better than his best friend?

I smile at Karen and say loudly, "Come on then, we don't want to keep Miss Rawlins waiting."

As we head to the car, I feel a prickle of excitement as I think about seeing Isabel this morning. I just know it will be ok, I can feel it in my heart.

I see her before she sees me and my heart starts thumping. She looks so beautiful in her pretty summer dress and hair hanging loose around her shoulders. She is laughing at something one of the other mother's is saying and I feel a surge of jealousy as I see the smile they share. Then she looks up and our eyes meet and her expression changes. It becomes wary and guarded and my heart sinks.

I watch as she excuses herself and heads over and looks with concern at Jamie. "Is everything alright?"

Jamie nods sullenly, and she raises her eyes to mine with unspoken questions in them. I say softly, "May I have a word in private, Miss Rawlins?"

She looks a little uncomfortable but Jamie's expression must tell her it concerns him and she nods. "Yes, follow me, we have a few minutes before the bell rings."

I bend down and straighten Jamie's jumper and tuck in his shirt, whispering, "It will be ok, trust me. I love you."

He nods and then runs off quickly with Jack and the tears threaten to fall as I see how brave he is being.

Isabel says gently, "Follow me, Tina."

As we walk towards the classroom, I feel my heart fill with hope. Seeing Isabel again has just reinforced the fact that I love her and want her in my life. I'm not sure why but she is a calm refuge in a storm. She soothes my troubles away with just one brief smile and I know that things are going to be ok.

We head inside the classroom and she closes the door and says coolly, "What's the problem?"

I smile tremulously, wishing she would just hold me and tell me everything will be ok and say sadly, "Harry left last night."

I watch her carefully for her reaction and my heart lifts as I see a flicker of excitement spark in her eyes before it's replaced with concern. "Left?"

"Yes, we've decided to separate, so Jamie is feeling sad and vulnerable."

She shakes her head and says sadly, "I'm so sorry to hear that. It's never nice where children are involved. Don't worry, I'll keep an eye out for him and offer him someone to talk to if he needs it. You did the right thing telling me."

I make to move towards her and she takes a step back. "Um… if that's all, I really should let the children in."

I stare at her in surprise. "I had hoped we could talk about what happened yesterday."

Sighing heavily, she looks at me with a sad expression. "I'm sorry, Tina. I should never have let myself get so involved. Things went too far and I'm sorry if I made you think there was more to our relationship than friendship. It was a mistake and can never happen again. Maybe we should just keep things on a professional footing as the teacher and parent from now on."

I stare at her in shock. "You don't mean that."

She looks at me with an ice-cold expression. "But I do, Tina. You see, I'm grateful that you were a friend when I needed one but that's all. To be honest, what we did disgusts me. I'm even finding it hard to look at you and I went home and scrubbed my skin bare just to remove any trace of you. You see, Tina, I could never love a person like you, anyway."

I step back as if she's slapped me. "What do mean, a person like me?"

Her eyes flash and it's as if she changes before my eyes as she snarls. "Look at you. Your child's father has just left and you're making eyes at me. Your child is suffering and yet all you can think of is dressing up and coming on to his teacher. You didn't give a second thought to Harry and Jamie all the time you were systematically destroying their lives and you turned your back on your best friend in favour of a stranger. Women like you are mad, Tina. Mad for chasing something that will never be theirs and turning their back on something amazing.

143

You had it all, and you took it and threw it away and for what? For nothing, absolutely nothing, so get out and never come to my classroom again."

I turn away blindly, trying desperately to erase the image of her staring at me with disgust. Then I move away quickly. I need to distance myself from her because this Isabel is a completely different person to the one I fell in love with. There was so much hate in her eyes and vitriol spilling from her lips like acid rain.

As I race back to my car, her words echo around my mind. She was ashamed over something I wanted to shout from the rooftops. She is disgusted over something beautiful and the hate that poured from her eyes and lips has destroyed me far more than Harry leaving. Isabel Rawlins has destroyed my life and I don't know how on earth I'm ever going to piece it back together again.

22

ISABEL

NINE MONTHS AGO

I feel so excited. I'm finally going on a date. I can't believe that things have worked out so well for me. Working with small children has many benefits but a social life isn't one of them. I've had the odd dates in the past but nothing that's ever worked out. Gradually the dates dried up, and I resorted to online dating websites and that's where I met Eddie.

As soon as I saw his profile, I knew we would get on. Not only is he gorgeous looking, totally my type, but he's funny as well.

So funny we talk for hours online. I think I know everything about him before he tentatively suggests meeting up.

My friend Carol warned me about meeting someone I don't know but I do know Eddie. He's my soulmate, I just know it.

I take extra care in getting ready because tonight, is going to be amazing. I run a deep, scented bath and soak for ages, making sure to shave all the important places. Then I do my make-up carefully and style my hair, before pulling on the silky lingerie I bought especially for the occasion. The final touch is to pull on a figure-hugging dress and climb onto my six-inch heels.

Standing back, I look at myself in the mirror with a critical eye and like what I see. Yes, Eddie Butler is in for a treat tonight.

At 7.30 sharp I walk into the local wine bar, Franklins. We agreed to meet here on neutral territory for a drink before heading out for a meal. To say I'm nervous is an understatement because this will be my first date in years. Unlike the usual boys that asked me out, Eddie is all man. I can tell from his profile picture and my heart starts thumping madly with nervous excitement.

I see him almost immediately. He is everything I thought he would be and more. He stands up as I approach and I can tell he likes what he sees, as do I because Eddie Butler is something else. Tall dark and handsome doesn't even do the man justice. He is drop dead gorgeous and I can't quite believe my luck.

He smiles as I approach and kisses me lightly on the cheek. His aftershave is intoxicating, much like the man himself and he says sweetly, "Isabel, we meet at last. You look amazing."

I smile shyly because although we have been talking for a couple of months, the reality is quite overpowering.

He pulls out the chair like a true gentleman and says lightly, "I've taken the liberty of ordering us some champagne. I hope that's ok with you."

He smiles and every part of me melts at that look. He is impressive.

As he hands me the glass, I say shyly, "It's good to meet you at last, Eddie. It feels as if it's been a long time coming."

He nods. "Yes, I suppose it's a good thing though. At least it means we know a lot about each other before the date."

He winks. "Although I must say if I knew you were quite so gorgeous, I wouldn't have waited this long."

His eyes hold mine and the intent in them has me gasping for breath. Yes, Eddie Butler wants me. It's all there in his eyes and I feel exactly the same.

Dinner is amazing. We talk, eat and get on like a house on fire. He is charming, funny and witty. He is also intelligent and I discover he went to university and studied accounting. This man is so perfect and I can't believe he's single.

After a while, I broach the subject of past relationships.

"You don't have to tell me if you don't want to but have you ever been in a long relationship, or um… married?"

He shakes his head sadly. "No. I was engaged once, but it never worked out. She left me for my best friend, so it was a difficult time."

Reaching out, I grasp his hand and say sympathetically, "I'm sorry, that must have been painful."

He grasps my hand tightly and rubs his thumb across it and I feel myself melting under his touch. His eyes glitter with passion as he says softly, "I'm glad."

"Glad?"

He smiles. "Because it enabled me to meet you."

My breath catches and I don't even care that it's a line he probably uses on everyone because I want Eddie so badly it hurts.

He smiles sexily and says softly, "Shall we get the bill?"

I swallow hard and nod because I know that Eddie wants me and I'm not going to say no. It's all there in his body language and expression. Licking my lips, I say huskily, "Yes, I think we should."

Eddie catches the waiter's attention and before I know it, we are hailing a cab and the driver says, "Where to guys?"

Eddie looks at me and his eyes glitter, "It's up to the lady."

I stare at him and drown in the desire in those compelling eyes and say huskily, "212 Indigo terrace."

The driver says cheerily, "Righto, I'll have you there in a jiffy."

The cab pulls away and Eddie pulls me close. His lips touch mine lightly as he whispers against mine, "Are you sure about this Isabel?"

Nodding, I push my lips to his and my kiss is all the answer he needs. At this point, I don't even care that we've technically just met and on the Internet at that. I don't think about the warnings I was given from everyone I know and some I don't about the perils of online dating. I don't think of anything but my basic needs that this man is about to satisfy for me. All of my intelligence has deserted me in a moment of blind lust.

Eddie and I hit my flat like a hurricane. As soon as we are inside the door, we are ripping each other's clothes off. It's fast, furious and frantic and I'm loving every minute of it. We are like wild animals as we devour each other. He slams me against the wall and kisses me all over. He pushes me to the floor as he enters me roughly. He pulls me on top of him as I claim him as mine. Then I scream out his name as he makes me come over and over again several times during the night, as we discover everything about each other until the dawn breaks.

Yes, Eddie Butler and Isabel Rawlins are compatible online and dynamite in person.

23

The next morning is just as frantic. Almost as soon as we wake up, we're hungry for each other again. Sex with Eddie was worth the wait. I'm making up for all those years when the only satisfaction I got was by my own hand. I am insatiable and so it appears, is Eddie.

We do manage to head out to lunch by the river Hamble and I feel myself glowing as I share a gorgeous lunch with an equally gorgeous man.

As soon as we return to my flat, we're at it again and I have never been so happy in my life.

However, it has to end as Eddie says regretfully, "I'm sorry, darling. I need to get back to London. I'm up early in the morning before the markets open."

I push down my disappointment and pull him against me. "I understand. I have to work too. When will I see you again?"

He pulls me tightly against him as if he never wants to let me go and says roughly, "I can't get away until Friday night. I'm sorry but work is so demanding and I can't take time out to meet you."

I nod in understanding and say lightly, "I could always come to London to see you. I don't know, maybe spend some time at yours."

He groans. "I wish you could but I work such long hours it wouldn't be fair. I also share a flat with a very annoying group of guys and I would never put you through that torture. No, Friday night will be good because it will give me the whole week to imagine what I am going to do to you when I return."

I feel a shiver run through me at his words. Sex with Eddie has been something else this weekend. He has introduced me to all kinds of things that I never thought I'd enjoy. It's been more like fifty shades of fun because we have done things I certainly don't want anyone else knowing about.

He kisses me deeply and I melt into him. I could make love to Eddie all day and all night because he is *that good*. How on earth am I going to last a whole week without him?

Sadly, I wave him off and set about tidying my flat. Grinning, I toss the sheets in the washing machine and remember the pounding they've taken this weekend. Then I call my friend Carol and relive the whole experience, minus the kinky stuff and then get myself ready for work. Maybe I do need a week to recover because I have never had a weekend like this one.

Outside of communicating online with Eddie, I do have a life to lead. My work at the local primary school is challenging and my evenings are spent marking and preparing lessons for the next day. I don't think there's anything odd about my relationship with him and as the weeks go by, all I think about is how much fun we have when he does come to stay.

I think it's three weekends later that I broach the subject of him meeting some of my friends.

We are lying in bed after another marathon session and I stroke his chest lightly. "Do you fancy going to a party later?"

He sounds surprised. "Where?"

Shifting, I look into his eyes and say with excitement, "My friend Carol's having a birthday party tonight and she's invited us to go. It will only be for a few hours and it may be fun and give me a chance to show you off."

He shakes his head sadly and pulls me to his lips. After kissing me gently, he sighs, "I'm sorry, darling. I have to return to London this evening."

I feel the disappointment washing over me. "Why?"

He groans. "There's an important meeting first thing on Monday morning. I'm going to need to be at my desk early on Sunday morning to prepare for it. I should have told you but as soon as I saw you my mind turned to other things."

He winks and I smile but feel the sadness behind it. He's leaving – early.

Trying to put on a brave face, I say with disappointment. "I'm sorry, that's a shame. You would have loved my friends."

He kisses me again and murmurs, "I know I would because you wouldn't spend time with anyone not worth liking."

Once again, we forget everything other than making the most of the last few hours we have and as I wave him off, I just feel sad that the weekend has ended so soon.

That evening I head to the party alone and Carol says in surprise, "Oh, I thought you were bringing Eddie."

Feeling a little awkward, I say apologetically, "He had to leave, I'm sorry, Carol, he sends his apologies."

She looks concerned. "I'm sorry, is everything ok?"

"Just his work. He's got such an important job it demands a lot of his time. Never mind, maybe we can catch up when he comes next time."

Carol nods but I don't miss the doubt in her eyes. I don't blame her; I'd be the same but I know Eddie and what we have is real. You can't fake the connection we share and it's just a shame we live so far apart.

As the weeks go by, I fall deeper and deeper in love with Eddie. He sends me flowers and chocolates and little cards filled with sentimental verses. We speak on the phone a lot and our face-time calls are purely x-rated. I have never felt as alive as I do when I'm with him and so when he suggests a night away in a plush hotel in the Lake District, I'm beside myself with excitement.

I meet him at Euston Station on Friday evening and as soon as I see him, I run into his arms. We kiss like any lovers would after not seeing each other for days and my heart soars as he takes my hand in his and says lovingly, "I've missed you, darling."

I couldn't be any happier than I am now and for the whole journey, we kiss and cuddle on the train in a carriage with few people to witness us. At one point, we even make our way to the toilets and join the equivalent to the mile-high club. Life just can't get any better than it is and I have never been so happy.

We are booked into a five-star luxury hotel with a spa at Lake Windermere. As we enter our room, I squeal with delight at the sight of the luxury four poster bed. Jumping onto it, I stretch out and groan with ecstasy. "This is amazing. I love it here."

Eddie joins me and we waste no time in christening the bed and by the time we make our way down to dinner, I feel the luckiest woman in the world.

However, my luck doesn't end there because amid the candlelight and champagne, Eddie produces a velvet-covered box and takes my hand in his, saying huskily, "Isabel Rawlins, I love you more than words can express and would be honoured if you would agree to be my wife."

I just stare at him in shock and my heart leaps. In fact, it thumps so hard I can almost hear it and as I drown in those sexy eyes, I say breathlessly, "Of course I will."

Eddie opens the box and slides an amazing diamond ring onto my finger and then pulls me across the table and kisses me lingeringly. Then he whispers, "You have made me the happiest man alive."

That night we eat like kings.

That night I have everything I ever wished for.

That night we pledge our souls to each other forever and that night we make love until the early hours.

That night I fall hopelessly and unequivocally in love with Eddie Butler and think I have the world.

That night I did have the world but unfortunately, it didn't last forever as I hoped. It didn't even last a month because three weeks to the day everything changed.

24

I'm not sure when the doubts started to creep in but like an unwanted fungus, they started seeping into the cracks. It must have been a week after our engagement that I broached the subject of meeting my family.

His answer set off the alarm bells.

"I'm sorry, darling. I would love to meet your family but I'm afraid I can only spend one evening with you this weekend and I don't think they would enjoy seeing what I have planned for you."

I stare at him with disappointment. "Why, what's so urgent you can't spend the weekend with me?"

He shakes his head and says sadly, "I'm afraid I'm working on a big project at work. I'm needed there on Saturday and Sunday if we have any hope of landing the bonus I'm counting on."

I feel irritable which is unlike me and say angrily, "It's not fair. I don't get to see you much and when I do, you can't stay long. Maybe I could come with you and wait in your flat. I don't know, I could take in the sights during the day and we could eat out at night."

He looks at me irritably. "I've told you before, it wouldn't work. I need every hour I can on this project and only go home to grab a few hours' sleep. I'm sorry, it can't be helped."

I turn away and he sighs heavily. "Listen, it won't be for much longer. If I get this bonus, it will set us up for life. It's worth a small fortune and will enable us to bring the wedding forward and even put down a deposit on a house. Trust me, darling. Of course, I would much rather meet your parents and spend a lovely weekend with you but in this instance, I can't."

I feel a little ashamed as he pulls me to him. "I'm sorry, darling. Please forgive me?"

I nod and he kisses me gently which makes everything better immediately.

Once again, sex takes priority and I make the most of it because if he's leaving tonight, it will be a full week before I see him again.

I'm not even sure why I did what I did next but after I wave him off, I head back into the bedroom and notice that he's left his watch on the bedside table. Without thinking, I grab hold of it and jump in my car, intending on meeting him at the station to return it. He's always insisted on getting a cab to the station which never really struck me as odd until I'm driving that way myself. Why I didn't just drop him there never occurred to me.

I pull up outside and head inside the ticket hall and look for the platform to London. I notice that it's on platform 1 and as I start heading that way, I catch sight of Eddie on the platform below. However, he is not on platform 1 to London, he's waiting on platform 3.

Looking up at the board, I notice it's heading to a different destination and the warning bells start ringing loud and clear. Without thinking, I purchase a ticket to the furthest destination on the route and hurry to the platform, making sure to keep out of sight. I feel a little bad for spying on him but it appears that curiosity has overpowered my sanity because I know in my heart something isn't right.

As soon as the train arrives, I take a seat by the window in the second carriage and Eddie sits in the first. As the train pulls out of Southampton, I have no idea where I'm going to end up.

As I wait, I spin the watch in my hands and notice an engraving on the back. TKJ. I wonder what that means, it's certainly not Eddie's initials?

Maybe it's a family heirloom or something because I know it's a good make. It may be quite valuable which doesn't surprise me because Eddie always dresses well and spoils me with expensive gifts. As my engagement ring catches the light, it flashes a warning at me. Should I be doing this? It's a bit crazy, really. It's almost as if I don't trust him but suddenly everything swirls around my head as I piece together the last few months. I think I know in my heart what I'm about to discover but I'm praying I'm wrong.

It must be an hour and a half later the train pulls into Surbiton. I see Eddie leave and scramble from my seat. I keep well back and position myself behind the crowd, keeping him in my sights all the time.

As I follow him from the station, I feel my heart thumping madly and I pray this isn't what I think it is.

He walks quickly and then takes a call. I hear him laughing and wonder who he's talking to. I don't even notice the smart houses that we pass or the tree-lined avenues. All I can concentrate on is the fact that my fiancé is somewhere other than where he said he was going.

It must be fifteen minutes later he turns into a smart road and heads toward a white house with shutters and an immaculate front garden. He passes through a little metal gate and I hear the hinge squeak in protest. I hide behind a tree and I see the door opens before he can get his key in the lock and a little boy races out. My breath catches as I see the little boy is the image of Eddie. He reaches down and swings the little boy in his arms and I hear the boy yell, "Mummy, daddy's home."

The tears blind my vision as I feel my heart breaking. Yes, Eddie Butler has been lying to me all along. He is married, and he does have a family. How could I have been so stupid?

I walk away.

I walk back along the same streets but I don't register where I am. All I can think of is that Eddie lied to me. He asked me to marry him when he was already married.

I head back to the station and wait for the train back to Southampton and think about everything that's happened over the last few weeks. Then I start making excuses for him. Maybe he does have a child but isn't with the mother. Perhaps they never married, and he was telling the truth. Could she be the one who left him for his best friend and was pregnant with his child? Maybe he didn't want to tell me because he was afraid it would drive me away.

As I travel home, these excuses become more believable with every passing mile. Maybe he is telling the truth and I'm thinking the worst of him. Perhaps he needed to go and see his son on his way home. These thoughts and many more besides keep me company on the journey home.

By the time I reach Southampton, I've decided to give Eddie the benefit of the doubt. I'll test the water when I see him next. One way or another, I'll get to the bottom of this once and for all.

25

Eddie phones me during the week and at the sound of his voice, my heart leaps. Despite the torture I've put myself through, I still crave him more than anything. After a few minutes, I say tentatively, "Um, you left your watch behind, did you notice?"

He groans. "So that's where I left it. Thanks, darling, I'll pick it up on Friday night."

"So, will you be staying for the whole weekend this time?"

There's a short pause, and he says, "I'm sorry, I can only manage a few hours this week. I'll make it up to you when this project's over, I promise."

Squeezing my eyes tightly shut to stop the tears from falling, I say in exasperation, "It's just not fair, can't you even stay the night?"

He says wearily, "Look, I know it's not the best but I can't help it. You will just have to be more understanding, Isabel. In fact, I shouldn't really see you on Friday evening but I want to see you so badly I'm risking it."

"Risking what?"

"Upsetting my boss. He wants me to meet him on Friday to go through a few things but I said I had a prior engagement. I'm sorry but you're a much more attractive proposition than he is so there was no comparison."

I can tell he's trying to lighten the mood and just say shortly, "Ok, Friday evening then."

He whispers, "I will make it up to you, I promise."

As he cuts the call, I throw my phone angrily onto the bed. I've had enough. I'm going to confront him on Friday night and find out just what's going on. I won't be made to look like a fool and be used if that's what he's doing. I have too much self-respect for that and come this Friday, Eddie Butler won't know what's hit him.

I'm not sure how I get through the next week. Eddie calls a few more times and I try to keep things normal. I'm not sure if he picks up on the edge in my voice, or that I don't appear as loving as always but I hope not. I want him to come on Friday and explain everything and I can't risk him cancelling.

Friday comes at last and as I wait, I feel nervous and apprehensive. My heart thumps along with every minute on the clock as I wait for his taxi to pull up outside. But it never does. When it comes to 8 pm I try calling but the phone just rings. There's no voicemail clicking in, just the endless ringing of a phone that's never answered.

I contemplate getting the train back to Surbiton when he doesn't call the next day. I feel so angry that he's just cast me aside because I'm not stupid. There's been no contact, nothing. It's too much of a coincidence, surely.

Then the worry takes over as by Sunday I've imagined all sorts. The only place I know he has a connection to is that house in Surbiton. It's agonising waiting for the phone to ring and any movement outside has me racing to the window to see if it's him.

Then I do get a call but it's not Eddie.

I see an unfamiliar number calling me and answer it quickly, "Isabel Rawlins."

"Good evening, Miss Rawlins. I'm sorry to trouble you. My name is Detective Inspector Matthews. I'm calling on behalf of an Eddie Butler."

My heart starts thumping and I say shakily, "Yes?"

"Can you confirm that you know an Eddie Butler?"

I swallow hard. "Yes."

"May I ask what relation you are to him."

I say shakily. "I'm his fiancée."

There's a brief pause and then his tone changes and he says kindly, "I'm sorry to ask but when was the last time you saw him?"

I don't falter. "Last Friday."

Again, there's a brief pause, and he says softly. "Please accept my apologies for this but may I ask, when was the last time you had contact with him?"

I say breathlessly, "Wednesday, around 5 pm. I'm sorry officer but why are you asking me all these questions, has something happened?"

There's another brief pause and then he says, "I'm sorry to do this over the phone but we have reason to believe that Eddie Butler has gone missing, presumed drowned."

I sit back in shock, the phone pressed to my ear, as the officer says, "Please can you tell me your address and I'll be right over. Maybe you can help us get to the bottom of this."

As I tell him what he needs to know, I feel my heart breaking inside. Presumed drowned. He can't be. There must be an explanation for this.

As I wait for the police officer to pay me a visit, I reign in my grief. Eddie isn't dead, I feel it in my heart. What the hell is going on?

26

As I watch the officer leave a few hours later my head spins with what he told me.

Eddie apparently left a suicide note among his clothes by a lake near Wimbledon. The officer told me that on further investigation they found he lived in a flat nearby. When they searched the property, they found hardly any personal possessions and just my phone number written on a pad next to the bed. The flat had been rented for six months which finished in one months' time. The letting company told them he said he needed it for work purposes and yet his neighbours said they only used to see him once a week. It all contradicts what I know about him and I wonder again, who is Eddie Butler?

I asked the officer if they knew of any family and he shook his head and said he'd been hoping I could provide them with more information. I was embarrassed to admit that I knew nothing about my fiancé and I could tell he pitied me and probably thought I was a gullible fool for dating a man off the Internet.

However, I didn't tell them about the house in Surbiton because if there's one thing I do know about this, it's that I'm going to carry out my own investigations on Eddie Butler and I think I know just where to find him.

It only took a few weeks to find the position at Highwood Primary school. My own school were sad I was leaving but understood when I told them I had to move for personal reasons. They never asked what they were which I was glad about. Revenge doesn't sit well on a Curriculum Vitae under 'other interests.'

I rented a flat close to the school and set about packing up what few possessions I had. As I went through the motions, I wrapped my broken heart in a ring of steel and prepared myself for a tough time ahead.

As I packed the watch, I resisted the urge to throw it against the wall. How dare he. How dare he play with me like this? To give me everything and then take it away with a lie. I feel so stupid but not anymore. From now on I'll be the one in control. I will call the shots and I will make him pay for what he did.

On the first day of school, I steeled myself to meet them. His family. I always knew his son would be in my class because I studied the register before I even took the job. As luck would have it, his teacher retired the term before and they were making do with a supply teacher.

I think my heart rate increased tenfold in the minutes before the playground opened. Maybe he would bring his child to school, Jack Mahoney. Yes, even then I knew his real name because I checked the addresses against the register and the address that I saw Eddie go to that day was the one that a Jack Mahoney lived at. He obviously lied about his name as well as everything else because Karen and Tom Mahoney are Jacks' parents. Maybe Jack is Eddie's son and Tom is someone else who his mother married. Maybe Eddie was telling the truth and I've got this all wrong. Well, I'm soon about to find out because if Eddie is Tom Mahoney, I'm going to find out and I can't wait to see his face when he sees me standing in front of him with his wife by his side.

However, Eddie doesn't accompany Jack to school. Instead, I see a pretty woman with kind eyes bringing two boys into school a little late. She smiles as I greet her and apologises for their lateness. I strike up a conversation and find nothing out of the ordinary, then again why would I? However, little Jack is the spitting image of Eddie, so I know I'm on the right track.

When I arranged the meetings with the parents, I had it all worked out. I would confront Eddie when he arrived with his wife and he would be forced to confess everything. However, she showed up alone and I was angry. The frustration consumed me and I didn't know what to do next. Then I was thrown a lifeline - the invitation to the barbeque was just what I needed because I was about to make him pay in front of all his friends and family.

I still remember the nerves when I walked up that familiar path, this time as an invited guest. Finally, I was going to find out once and for all.

However, nothing prepared me for what happened next. As I caught sight of Eddie across the garden, the world stood still. It was *him* - Eddie. He was laughing at something someone said to him as Tina pointed him out to me.

My heart raced as we walked towards him and I felt sick. Then our eyes met and I would have my moment of revenge. However, the eyes that met mine were like a strangers. They were polite and curious but it was obvious he didn't remember me.

I was shocked and didn't know what to do next. He was polite and courteous and when his wife appeared by his side, I felt the jealousy consume me as I saw the love he had for her reflected in his eyes. They all looked at me with concern because quite frankly, I was speechless.

Eddie is Tom and Tom is Eddie. It's obvious. Tom has a beard where Eddie did not but I could see it clearly. It was no coincidence that Eddie walked up that path and the little boy called him daddy. It was no coincidence that Eddie lived in a rented temporary apartment because he had a home here and it was no coincidence that Eddie fabricated his own death to get him off the hook when I started getting suspicious. However, what I don't understand is how he can pretend so well that he has never seen me before.

It took a few more days before I found about his attack. He was mugged on his way home from work and that must have caused some kind of trauma to his head. It can be the only explanation because even I know he's not that good an actor.

I even tried to force the issue by telling Karen about the watch. Apparently, all it did was make him agitated and bring back bad memories of that night. Either that or he's using it as an excuse and is pretending this whole time.

So, as the weeks turned to months, I was resigned to waiting it out until Tom's memory returned because what we had, the future I was promised, was too good to give up on.

The trouble is, now things are complicated because something happened and then Tina became a problem I never saw coming.

27

KAREN

I think I'm in shock. Harry's left. I can't quite take it all in and as soon as they leave for school, I ring Tom.

"Hey, baby. Is everything ok?"

"Not really. Did you know that Harry's left?"

"What do you mean, left?"

"Packed his bags and left. Jamie's devastated and Tina, well, I don't know, really."

Tom sounds shocked. *"What do you mean you don't know?"*

"She seemed almost normal and was dressed up smartly looking as if she was going on a night out, rather than devastated that her partner's just left her."

"That's terrible. I'll give Harry a call to see if he's ok."

"Ok, let me know if I can help in any way."

"Sure, see you later - love you."

"Love you too."

Throughout the day, Tina and Harry are all I can think about. I leave work a little early in the hope of grabbing a bit of time with her. She will need me to be a good friend during the coming weeks, not to mention Jamie.

I suppose I should have seen this coming because all the warning signs were there. By their own admission, their sex life wasn't great. I saw the irritable glances and heard the snide remarks but just put it down to them going through a rough patch because of the baby issue. I'm pretty sure that Isabel's offer can't have helped the situation and I worry for my friend.

I feel a little nervous as I knock on the door and am surprised when Tina opens it looking absolutely terrible. Her eyes are red-rimmed from crying and her face pale and tight. She nods as I follow her in and calls to the boys, "It's ok, Jack, you can stay for a bit longer. I'll have a cup of tea with your mum first."

We hear, "Ok" and as I reach the kitchen, she closes the door and collapses into a sobbing heap at the table.

Rushing over, I put my arm around her shoulders. "It's ok, let it all out. It's ok to cry."

She shakes her head and mumbles. "You don't understand."

I sit beside her and say gently. "It's ok. You don't have to tell me but I'm a good listener."

173

Wiping her eyes, she blows her nose into a tissue and stares at me with a blank look. "I've been such a fool."

I say nothing and she shakes her head. "I've ruined everything."

"I'm sure it will be ok. Maybe you just need to talk it through, find some common ground and take things slowly."

Her eyes are filled with pain as she sniffs, "I'm not sure that's possible."

I smile reassuringly. "Anything's possible if you want it badly enough."

She nods, "I do, I want it more than anything but I've ruined everything."

Standing up, I reach for the kettle and say firmly, "Come on, I'll make you some tea and you can calm down for a minute. I'll take Jamie home with us for tea and maybe you can call Harry and talk this all out."

I'm not sure I hear her right because the water is filling the kettle when she says, "It's not Harry I'm worried about."

Plugging in the kettle, I turn and say, "Sorry, what did you say?"

She stares at me as if she's seeing a ghost and whispers, "It's Isabel."

"Isabel?"

I feel the anger rushing through me. Of course, Isabel. I say tightly, "Are you telling me that Isabel's the reason why you and Harry have split up. I knew she was trouble."

Tina sniffs. "You don't understand. It's not Harry."

Feeling a little impatient, I say carefully. "Tell me so I can understand."

She looks a little embarrassed. "I think I love Isabel; in fact, I know I do."

I stare at her in complete shock. "What do you mean?"

"I think I've developed feelings for Isabel and thought she felt the same."

"Why do you think that?"

"Because we became good friends and when you were away, she stayed the night."

I'm not sure I want to hear the answer but I have to ask, "What do you mean, stayed the night? Like in a sleepover type of way?"

Tina blushes and I stare at her in shock. "You mean, you and Isabel…"

She nods and I sit down heavily. "Oh"

She starts to cry again and then says with pain in her voice. "It was amazing, Karen. I have never felt like that with anyone before. It's as if everything made sense all of a sudden. I was so happy and when Harry came back, I couldn't bear the thought of him touching me."

Feeling a little faint, I say softly, "Does Harry know, is that why he left?"

She shakes her head and sobs. "No, he just thinks we should split because things haven't been right for a long time. I was so cold with him when he got back and couldn't wait to see the back of him."

The shock must show on my face because she nods. "I know, I'm a bitch but I couldn't see past my need for Isabel."

I have to know and say tightly, "What about Isabel, what's the situation there?"

My question brings with it a fresh bout of tears as Tina sniffs, "She doesn't want me and told me it was a mistake and that what we did... um... disgusts her. She was so cold, Karen and told me to leave her alone."

Despite everything I've heard, I feel so much compassion for Tina. I can see she is devastated and my heart aches for her.

Moving across, I take her in my arms and hug her tightly. "There, there, it's ok. Things aren't that bad. I'm sure we can work it out."

Pulling back, she cries, "I just want *her*. I just want her to admit she wants me and to come and live with me and Jamie. I want us to be a family and have one of our own. I just want that; does that make me a bad person, Karen?"

I think that last statement shocks me more than anything else I've heard. As I look at my friend, I don't see the woman I've known for close on ten years. This woman is a stranger to me and I stare at her in horror. Not knowing what to do, or say, I take the cowards way out and just say firmly, "You need to think about this. Let me take Jamie for a sleepover tonight and you can think it all through. Maybe give Harry a call, I don't know, watch a film, anything to get some kind of normal back into your life. Maybe Tom will look after the boys and we could sit here and talk about it, maybe grab a pizza and go through it all. What do you say?"

Tina looks as if she has the world on her shoulders as she nods gratefully. "Thanks, Karen. It's a kind offer and you're right, maybe Jamie would be better off at yours. I'll take a rain check on the talk though. I think I'm just going to get an early night instead."

She stands and heads to the kitchen door and shouts, "Jamie, do you want to stay at Jack's tonight?"

"Yes, please mum. Can I take my game?"

Tina looks at me and I nod. She shouts, "Ok but only play on it for an hour."

She closes the door and smiles gratefully. "Thanks, Karen. You know, I think I just need to sleep and try to process what's happened and I really appreciate this."

As she heads across and makes the tea, I worry about her. She looks lost and broken and by the sounds of it, she's not going to like the ending of this particular saga. All I can do is to be there for her and be the friend she needs right now. Maybe this will all blow over and be the best thing that ever happened to them. I hope so for all their sakes.

As I think about Isabel, my heart hardens. I always knew that woman was trouble and I'm betting she had a hidden agenda in all of this. Maybe I should be the one to pay her a visit and find out just what she's up to.

28

As soon as the boys are in bed, I fill Tom in on what I know. He looks as shocked as I was and shakes his head. "I can't believe it. Do you think Harry knows?"

"I don't know, did you speak to him today?"

He nods. "Briefly. Work was mad and Harry took ages to return my call. He's staying at a friend's place until he decides what's happening. I feel sorry for him, especially after what you've just told me."

I nod. "I know, to be honest, my sympathies are with him in all this and Jamie, of course. Tina is acting so out of character, it's just not like her. I don't know what's happened to make her, so – well, crazy actually."

Tom looks at me thoughtfully. "Do you think it's the result of being told she can't have any more children?"

I shrug. "Possibly. Grief affects people in different ways. I can't believe Isabel though. I never saw this one coming."

Tom nods and I look at him sharply. I'm not sure why but I can't shake off the feeling that he knows Isabel more than he's letting on. Maybe it's the watch, or maybe it the story she told but I think back to how we were before the accident and it wouldn't surprise me.

Our life was very different then to what it is now. Tom stayed out a lot always saying it was work, and he was using the flat in town. He was withdrawn, irritable and moody. He always seemed as if he was carrying a huge burden and had the weight of the world on his shoulders. He never had time for us and I always put it down to the fact he had never wanted children. I trapped him and I'll freely admit it because my need for Jack overshadowed his needs.

I'm not proud of the fact I deceived him into thinking I was still on the pill but I'd do it again if it meant I had Jack. I can sort of understand Tina's need for a baby because after all, I've been down that particular road myself. However, Tom wasn't Harry who always seemed to love Tina a little too much. She was quite rude to him in public and used to treat him terribly at home. She was always dismissive of him and used to joke about his stamina on nights out. I would never treat anyone the way Tina used to treat him and I'm not surprised their relationship has suffered.

Thinking about my own relationship, I remember how different it is now. Tom was always a confident lover and sometimes he was a little too adventurous for my liking. I suppose it used to anger him that I wouldn't try out his little fantasies and subsequently sex became less often. After Jack, it was virtually never and so when Isabel pitched up with his watch, it just reinforced what I knew all along.

The one thing that concerns me ironically is that he doesn't appear to recognise her at all. Maybe the knock on his head has had serious repercussions and we should get him checked out. It's true he's been different since that night but I can't put my finger on it. Less aggressive, kinder and more attentive. I wonder what really happened that night because Tom came home very different from how we went out.

As I look over at him, I smile. He's watching a documentary on climate change and is biting his bottom lip like he always used to. Occasionally, he looks up and smiles and then resumes his concentration. My love knows no limits for Tom Mahoney and I thank god he wasn't seriously hurt that night. I just hope that Tina will be half as lucky as me because everyone deserves a man like Tom in their life – don't they?

As I get ready for bed, I wonder if I should check on Tina. I would hate to think of her crying herself to sleep but I can see the lights are out so she must have had an early night.

Tom comes up behind me and wraps his arms around me tightly, whispering, "Promise me we will never be Harry and Tina. I couldn't bear it if you left me."

Spinning around, I look up at him and smile. "That would never happen."

I don't know why the flash of uncertainty that sparks in his eyes makes me worry. I know he's hiding something. I've known for years he has a secret, I just never wanted to find out what it was. Tom was always the type of guy who kept his cards close to his chest. One minute he was up, then down like a gambler or drug addict. As he kisses me slowly and I feel the familiar stirring of lust, I push the doubts away as I always do. Whatever he did is in the past now, it's our future that matters and I will never let anything come between us and protect it with everything I've got.

The morning comes and I have two extremely reluctant boys to get off to school. I feel a little guilty that they stayed up way past their bedtime but I thought that Jamie could use the distraction.

He doesn't say anything, but it's written all over his face that he's suffering and I make sure to serve him a little more cereal than normal to give him energy for the day ahead.

As soon as I drop the boys into the playground, I look around for Isabel. I don't see her and approach a teacher nearby.

"Oh, hi Mrs Armstrong, I can't seem to see Miss Rawlins."

She shakes her head. "No, she's taken some time off, apparently, she's feeling unwell."

"Oh, I'm sorry to hear that. Wish her well if you see her."

Mrs Armstrong is distracted and I head to my car. My showdown with Isabel will have to wait until she's back but I'm determined to find out what she's playing at, even if I don't like what she says.

29
TINA

My head is hammering and my mouth is dry.
The tears dried long ago on my face and I groan as
the hammering in my head reminds me what a fool I
was last night.

If I could go to sleep and never wake up again, I
would. I try not to think of what I did last night but
the memory taunts me. When Karen took Jamie, I
did as I said I would. I had a nice warm bath and
made myself feel slightly more normal. Then it
struck me that it would be a bad idea to stay in on
my own, so I decided to go out instead. I had a
foolish notion that I would find Isabel in the wine
bar around the corner from the gym, so I made
myself look as pretty as I could and hopped in a cab
to take me there.

As I sat there alone at the bar it became
increasingly obvious, she wasn't coming. All
around me were people having a good time except
for me. I suppose I had too much to drink because
when a guy sat next to me, I started to chat to him
despite the fact I could see what he was after. His
gaze lingered on my chest and I noticed his eyes
running the length of my thigh as I crossed my legs.

Maybe it was because he was flattering me, or giving me some much-needed attention but when he suggested I accompany him to his hotel nearby, I did.

Groaning, I pull the pillow over my head as if to block out the memory of what we did. Almost as soon as we set foot inside his hotel room, we were at it. I was just as bad as him and left any inhibitions I had firmly at home. Maybe it was the alcohol and maybe it was because I was feeling so rejected but I behaved like an animal. Maybe it was because I wanted to prove I still liked men and wanted to see if it was men in general and not just Harry that turned me off.

Well, I found that particular answer out and went at it like a well-seasoned pro, which is just what he made me feel like. As soon as we finished, he rolled off of me and left the bed, returning with a wad of notes which he laid beside me. He told me to call a cab and keep the change and then he winked. *He winked*, and I felt so mortified I grabbed the cash and ran.

As the memory taunts me, for some reason, I start laughing uncontrollably. What is happening to me? I'm unravelling like a thread caught in a locked door. If I don't get a grip, there will be nothing left of me to cover my shame. I am a car crash, a wreck and an accident waiting happen and in the cold light of day, I vow to get the help I need. However, first of all, I need coffee and fast.

As I wait for the kettle to boil, there's a knock on the door and I look at the clock. 10 am. Feeling a little worried that it may be Jamie, I can't believe that I didn't ring Karen to check on him. I rush to the door and fling it open feeling worried. However, it's not Karen but Harry and he looks so angry I can almost taste it.

Pushing past me, he heads to the kitchen and I say airily, "Well, come in why don't you?"

He looks me up and down and I feel ashamed. My hair's a mess and I still have the remnants of last night's make-up on my face. I can pretty much guess that I look like a complete lush with red-rimmed eyes and puffy cheeks.

Pulling my robe a little tighter, I say angrily, "You don't get to barge in here without phoning first. I'm not in any fit state to deal with this right now."

He shakes his head in disbelief. "You're right about that. Look at you, you're a mess."

Suddenly, I remember he shouldn't be here and say urgently, "What is it, is it Jamie, please god no?"

He looks at me with pity. "No, it's not our son who is safely tucked up at school where he should be. Thanks for checking though, at least you can remember you have a son."

I shout. "How dare you? I'm a good mother, in fact, a much better mother than you are a father. I mean, what kind of father deserts his son one night and then doesn't come around to check on him the next day? Tell me, I'd love to know."

Harry looks as if he's about to smash something and then appears to shake himself and says in a cold voice. "For your information, I've seen Jamie every day. I meet him at lunchtime and take him out for a meal. We talk about things and he knows where he can reach me if he needs to talk."

I stare at him in surprise. "I never knew, Jamie never said."

"I'm not surprised because from what I understand, you haven't spent a lot of time with him since I left."

I laugh dully. "You left less than a week ago, so we're hardly talking months here. Anyway, why have you come here, Harry?

He smiles ruefully. "I wanted to check that you were ok. I know our split was inevitable but I'm not cold enough to walk away without checking on you."

I stare at him and for a moment wish things could have been different for Harry and I. He's a good man and made a fantastic partner. The trouble is, I took him for granted and gradually fell out of love with him. The excitement went when real life took over. I was always so tired and obsessing over being the perfect mother and housewife, I kind of forgot to be the woman he deserved.

Sitting down, I say sadly. "I'm sorry."

He sits opposite and says gently. "You have nothing to be sorry about. I suppose we both changed and have to take an equal share of the blame."

Seeing him sitting in front of me feels so familiar and safe. It makes me wonder why I can't just be happy with what I've got. A lovely son and a loving partner. Why did I feel the need to put stress on our relationship by wanting a baby so badly?

Harry sighs heavily. "Look, I also came to tell you I've been offered a job in Milton Keynes. It's a temporary contract for six months and I think I should take it."

I stare at him in confusion. "But what about Jamie, how will that work?"

"It's fine. He can come and stay at weekends and holidays. I'll make sure to come and collect him on Friday nights and drop him back on Sundays, if he wants to that is."

I feel strangely annoyed and snap, "I don't think you've thought this through. Jamie needs stability at the moment. What about football and his clubs and interests? You'll be dragging him away from his friends and hobbies to sit with you in a crummy bedsit. No, I don't think this is a good idea at all."

Harry looks at me angrily. "Then what do you suggest, I hang around here and put my life on hold while you have some sort of midlife crisis?"

"Midlife crisis, is that what you think this is? You think I'm mad, don't you? Well, that's typical and the reason why we could never work. You don't understand me and you never have done. Well, fine, you go off and start a new life in Milton Keynes and make your poor son suffer the consequences. You're selfish, Harry, always have been and always will be."

Without a word, Harry stands and moves towards the door and I shout after him. "That's it, run away. Walk away from your problems like you always do. Don't expect me to care though because I stopped caring a long time ago."

He slams the door on his way out and I stare after him in disbelief. Milton Keynes. He's deluded if he thinks that's a good idea.

I feel so angry; I start cleaning like I always do when I want to think. This may be a terrible situation to be in but I thought he would at least try to make it as easy on Jamie as possible.

Once I finish cleaning, I set about making myself look presentable. If Harry can move on this quickly, so can I. It's about time I got myself a job because by the sounds of things, I'm going to need one and I know just the place to start looking. In fact, it's the perfect solution and I'm surprised I never thought of it before.

30

The receptionist looks up at me and smiles. I return her smile although mine is a nervous one.

"Um… I was wondering if the opening was still available for a teaching support assistant?"

The receptionist smiles and looks at her computer screen. "Yes, applications close tomorrow. Do you have a current CV you could leave?"

I shake my head, feeling stupid. "No, I'm sorry."

She prints something out and hands it to me, saying kindly, "Don't worry, fill in this application form and you can drop the CV in later."

I take the form and sit down and start to fill it in.

It's been ages since I applied for a job and some questions take me by surprise. However, I really need this job because I won't be able to rely on Harry to support me for much longer. However, I know the real reason is Isabel. I could work in the same place as her, maybe even in the same classroom. We would see each other every day and she may just realise we are meant to be together.

Feeling a lot brighter now I've made a decision, I hand my application form in and say with interest, "When do you think I'll hear?"

She shrugs. "I'm not sure, maybe next week. It would be good if you could get your CV ready and handed in soon though, there has been a lot of interest."

Feeling upbeat, I say with a smile, "I'll head home now and do just that. Thank you."

As I turn to leave, I say almost as an afterthought, "Um… I don't suppose Miss Rawlins is available for a quick chat about my son Jamie Sears?"

Shaking her head, the receptionist looks apologetic. "I'm sorry, Miss Rawlins is currently signed off as sick. You can speak to the supply teacher if it's urgent."

Pushing down my disappointment, I smile ruefully, "No problem. I'll catch up with her when she's back."

As I walk away, I feel a little worried about Isabel. Maybe she is suffering and could do with someone to look after her. Impulsively, I reach for my phone and text her.

Hey, Isabel. I heard you're feeling unwell. Would you like me to bring anything over and look after you? xx

I feel a little anxious after the last text she sent but she may have calmed down by now. However, this time the message pops up as undeliverable.

I stare at it in shock. This can't be right. It's her number, why won't it work?

I check the number again and try once more. It may be due to a weak signal or something. It comes back the same, so I dial the number. This time a recording tells me the number is not available and a feeling of dread fills me. Turning around, I walk back to the main office and say rather sharply, "Please, do you have Miss Rawlins telephone number? For some reason, the number I have for her is unobtainable. I just wanted to wish her a speedy recovery."

Shaking her head, the receptionist looks a little uncomfortable. "I'm sorry, we aren't allowed to give out personal numbers for our staff. Maybe you should write a card and drop it in and we'll see that she gets it."

I smile thinly and turn away as it hits me, of course, I'll just drop around to her flat. What's the worst that could happen? I mean, she may just ignore the knock or then again, she may be pleased to see me.

I head towards her flat stopping briefly to buy her a bunch of flowers to cheer her up.

As I turn into her road, I feel the nerves flutter inside me as I wonder how she'll react. I hope in a positive way because even if she doesn't want anything other than friendship, that's fine by me. At least we could be good friends if all else fails.

Nervously, I approach the communal entrance and press the number on the entry system. It buzzes for ages but there's no answer. Stepping back, I look up at her window and see nothing but the curtains pulled neatly back from the window. I try again and still nothing until a lady opens the door and says politely, "May I help you?"

I say anxiously, "Possibly, I'm visiting Isabel Rawlins. There's no answer, and I heard she's ill so I'm a little worried."

The woman looks surprised. "But Isabel moved out two days ago. I thought she would have told you."

Her words are a blow to my sanity and I feel a huge wave of desolation threatening to pull me under.

Isabel has gone.

Shaking my head, I try to think on the spot and say breathlessly, "Do you have a forwarding address, or know where she went?"

"No love. I'm sorry she never said. Maybe the letting agents in the high street know something. I know they are responsible for renting out the flat, maybe they can tell you."

Thanking her, I head back to my car and fling the flowers in the back without care. As I sit behind the wheel, I know this is the end for me and Isabel. She's left. She's changed her phone and her address and doesn't want me to find her. She may be sick from school but I doubt she'll return.

As I come to terms with rejection, I slump over the steering wheel and sob like a baby. My life is meaningless. The only positive thing in it is Jamie, and I have disregarded his emotions in all of this in favour of my own. I'm a terrible mother and a terrible person.

As the grief hits me hard, so does the realisation that I've been a fool. I have thrown away everything good in my life for a pipe dream. The only thing I want to do now is to get my life back, and that means grovelling on my hands and knees to Harry and begging him to come home.

On the drive home, I have it all worked out. I'll cook him his favourite meal and make sure I look amazing. I'll ask Karen to look after Jamie and then I'll remind Harry just how good we are together.

Feeling brighter at the thought I can repair what I've torn down so cruelly, I head to the shops to buy the ingredients. By the time I get home, I feel good about things and dash off a couple of quick texts.

The first one is to Karen

Hey, sorry to ask again so soon
but can you mind Jamie this evening?
I need to have a heart to heart with Harry xx

The second is to Harry himself.

Hey, babe. Listen I'm sorry about earlier.
I was a bitch and we need to talk about
this like mature adults. How about you
come home this evening for tea and
we'll talk it through? Xx

Karen's is the first reply.

No problem. Just call me when you
want him back if not he can stay the night.
I hope it goes well. Xx

Harry's text comes almost at the same time.

What time?

I text back and arrange it for 6.30 and now it's
settled I feel positive for the first time in ages.
Maybe Harry was right, and I was having a mid-life
crisis. However, now it's time to face the facts and
put this all behind me. There will be no baby, no

Isabel and no job in Milton Keynes. Tonight, I am going to show Harry just how much he means to me because tonight, I am going to ask him to marry me.

31
KAREN

I think about Tina's text and wonder if she's seen sense at last. I certainly hope so because it's obvious she's losing her mind a little and going through a sort of crisis. I feel so sorry for Jamie and Harry being caught up in the whole sorry saga and think about what Tina told me about Isabel.

So, it's with considerable surprise that I read the next text that flashes in my Inbox, it's from Isabel.

Hi, Karen. I'm sorry to ask you this but please could you spare me an hour of your time? I am in town this afternoon and could meet you for lunch if you're free. Isabel x

I stare at the text and feel a little apprehensive. There is so much that has been left unsaid and I'm pretty sure that this is no cosy get together. Whatever Isabel wants to say is going to be hard to hear. However, curiosity wins and I text back.

Yes, of course. I'll meet you at Costa

near Marks and Spencer's. My
lunch is at 1 pm is that ok?

Yes, great, I'll see you there.
Oh, and Karen, please don't tell
Tina about this, I need to see you
alone.

I realise she doesn't know that I know about her night spent with my friend and I expect she's about to tell her side of the story. However, I have questions of my own that require answers and she may not like what I have to say.

1 o'clock comes and I head quickly to Costa. I see Isabel waiting just inside the door and she nods as I approach. She looks tired and anxious, completely different to how she usually does and I can tell something is troubling her.

She smiles weakly. "Let me buy the drinks while you find a seat. What can I get you?"

"Um, a latte please, but let me pay for it."

Waving away my money, she says with determination. "No, my treat, I insist."

I choose a seat at the rear of the coffee shop that gives us a little privacy and wonder what she has to say. She looked almost defeated as she stared at me. I'm not sure why but at that moment, Isabel looked vulnerable and I wonder what's wrong. It must be what happened with Tina.

As I see her approaching, balancing the tray of drinks, I harden my heart. No, Isabel needs to explain herself and I will not be swayed by this act she has going on.

She sits down and pushes the drink towards me and looks apologetic. "I'm sorry about this. I know you don't have long so I'll get straight to the point."

I say nothing but feel my heart thumping inside. There's a look in her eye that I've never seen before. She's always appeared so self-assured, so in control and a little cold but the woman sitting in front of me is none of those things. Her eyes are filled with tears and she says sadly, "I just wanted you to know that they've found Eddie."

Of all the things I thought she was going to say, it wasn't this. As I stare at her in shock her face falls, and she sniffs, "I found out two days ago. His body was found, and they identified it as him. I'm sorry if I gave you cause to doubt your own relationship with Tom. It must have just been a coincidence; he must have a double out there."

Shaking my head, I feel sudden compassion for her and reaching out, take her hand in mine. "Are you ok?"

She smiles sadly. "It's a relief if I'm honest. I suppose I've been in limbo for a while and I really thought Eddie was Tom. There were just too many coincidences to ignore."

Leaning back, I nod in agreement. "I thought so too. You see, when you were supposed to have been seeing Eddie, things with Tom and I were rocky. In fact, that's too mild a term for where we were heading. I always thought he was having an affair but could never prove it. I suppose I've always been expecting that knock on the door or the phone call and when you arrived all my worst fears were confirmed. I'm sorry to hear about Eddie, was it drowning as you thought?"

I feel bad for asking when the tears spill onto the table. Wiping them away, she sniffs, "Yes. They found his body in the lake. The funeral is next week and so I've decided to head home. I've left my job at the school and have taken another one."

She laughs as she sees my expression. "I know you think I'm a fast worker but quite honestly things have become… shall we say, difficult for me here."

I nod and she sighs. "I can tell you know about, Tina, I wouldn't have expected you not to. The trouble is, I just wanted friendship because as you know, I don't have many. That night was unexpected and things got a little out of hand. I didn't expect to wake up next to Tina and I can't deal with what we did. I need to move away and start again and think that's the best for everyone. Please don't tell Tina, at least until after I've left."

Feeling a little uncomfortable, I smile weakly. "I'm sorry for everything. I didn't think highly of you because I thought you were the 'other woman.' I thought you had come here to ruin my marriage, and I didn't trust you. Tina is vulnerable at the moment and I suppose I thought you were taking advantage of that."

Reaching across the table, I hold out my hand and as she takes it, I squeeze it and say softly, "I'm sorry for not being the friend you wanted and I'm sorry for what has happened both with Eddie and Tina. I wish you well though and hope the future is brighter."

Suddenly, Isabel smiles and her face totally transforms. She looks as if all the troubles she has faded away in an instant and she smiles mysteriously. "My future is bright, Karen. You don't need to worry about me, I have everything I came here for and more. I have closure and that means everything. Now I'm about to embark on another journey and this one promises to be everything I've ever wished for."

I notice the time and say apologetically, "I'm so sorry Isabel, I need to get back. I appreciate you telling me though, you didn't have to."

She smiles. "I did. Don't think badly of me, Karen. We're all looking for the same things in life. A loving family and a happy life. Some are luckier than others and find it sooner rather than later.

Others have to work at it a little harder. Mine is out there, I just know it."

As we part company at the door, I wonder what the future holds for Isabel. I hope it's a better one than the last year because underneath it all, she seems nice and would make a lovely wife and mother for some lucky guy.

As I make my way back to work, it's with a new spring in my step. So, Tom wasn't the one. He didn't cheat on me with Isabel at least and the watch must have been bought from whoever mugged Tom. If Eddie mugged Tom, he paid the highest price for his sins.

Now all I want to do is put this all behind me and concentrate on helping Tina save her relationship.

32
TINA

I feel so nervous waiting for Harry. I shouldn't because we have been together for so long now, I know him better than I know myself, obviously.

The things I have done lately have been so out of character I think I must have been having a breakdown. The whole Isabel thing still hurts and I can't deny I had very real feelings for her. However, that ship has sailed as they say and I need to move on and put things right.

I check the dinner and feel happy that it all looks and smells amazing. I've cooked Harry's favourite dish and tidied up making the house look cosy and inviting. I have taken extra special care with my appearance and worn the dress I know he likes the most. There are lit candles on every surface and the soft sound of his favourite album playing in the background. I've also changed the sheets and made the bedroom look seductive and inviting by lighting candles and positioning two glasses next to a bottle of champagne in an ice bucket by the bed.

Thinking of the sexy lingerie I bought for the occasion, I feel my heart flutter at the thought of what may happen later. If Harry agrees to marry me, I will be the perfect wife. I won't want another child and just take care of the one I have.

Jamie is safely at Karen and Tom's for the night and tomorrow I will begin the process of making it up to him. However, tonight is mine and Harry's and as the doorbell rings, I can't get to open the door quickly enough.

My heart lifts as I see him standing nervously on the step and I smile. "Come in, thanks, for meeting me."

He shrugs and looks apprehensive as he follows me into the kitchen.

He looks a little surprised when he sees the effort I've gone to and I smile softly, saying huskily, "Would you like a glass of champagne, Harry?"

He looks confused. "What for?"

Taking a deep breath, I just say mysteriously, "All will be revealed over dinner."

My fingers shake as I pour him a glass and as I hand it to him, our fingers touch and I feel the shivers inside. Yes, Harry is a good-looking man and I appear to have lost sight of that lately. Tonight, he is dressed in his suit that he obviously wore to work and his hair is slightly messy on top and his eyes weary.

Pulling out the chair, I say warmly, "Make yourself at home, you can always shower and change if you like. Your clothes are just where you left them."

He raises his eyes and says wearily, "What's this all about, Tina? I got your message and thought it was Jamie. Where is he by the way?"

"Don't worry about him, he's fine and spending the night at Jack's."

I laugh nervously. "We have the whole night and the house to ourselves. I thought we could talk about things and where we go from here."

He nods and sits down heavily on the kitchen chair. "Yes, I think we need to sort this out."

"Not before dinner though. You must be starving, so I've made you your favourite, lamb shanks."

He looks surprised. "You didn't have to go to so much trouble. I could have grabbed a takeaway on the way home."

I wince at his choice of word. Home. He is already thinking of somewhere else as home and he's only just left.

As I dish up the meal, I try to think about how I can broach the subject. Do I just come out and say it, or should I see where the conversation goes first?

I hand him his plate and sit opposite him, saying brightly, "Isn't this nice, just like old times?"

He smiles wearily. "Yes, I suppose it is."

I start by asking him about work, thinking it's common ground, and he says awkwardly, "I should maybe pack a little more of my things while I'm here. The job starts next week and I probably won't be able to get away easily to fetch the rest of them."

Taking a deep breath, I say nervously, "Um… as you've mentioned it, I just um… wanted to say… that is…"

He looks wary and I blurt out, "Please don't leave, Harry."

He looks surprised. "What do you mean, I have to, the contract's been signed? If it's Jamie, you're worried about, we've discussed it and he's more than happy to visit on weekends. I made sure of that before I agreed to it."

Feeling frustrated, I set my plate aside and feel the tears welling up in my eyes. "I don't want you to go to Milton Keynes and I don't want you to go back to that place you're staying. I want you to come home and be with us again where you belong."

Reaching out, I take his hand and say emotionally, "I want you, Harry. Not another baby, not another woman, not another man, just you. You see, I've discovered I can't live without you and I want to say… um… will you marry me, darling?"

The shock in his eyes makes me swallow hard, and he pulls away as if he's been burnt and says roughly, "What did you just say?"

Smiling, I move towards him and pull him close, resting my head on his chest like I always used to and murmur, "I want us to get married. I know we've always said it's not necessary for us but I want us to make that commitment. You see, you are my soulmate, darling and it's taken what happened with Isabel to make me see that. It's you I love and I want us to be that special couple again; that special family we always were."

I'm surprised when Harry pushes me away angrily and says in anger, "What happened with Isabel?"

I stare at him in confusion. "I'm sorry what did you say?"

He speaks slowly, "What. Happened. With. Isabel?"

Nervously, I swallow hard and say in a small voice, "I didn't mean for it to happen. I suppose I was a little obsessed and read too much into my feelings for her. When she offered to be our surrogate, I was so happy I think I confused things in my mind and that night you went camping with Jamie we sort of…"

"What?"

The tears spill as I sob, "We slept together."

There is silence and I almost can't look at him and when I do, I wish I hadn't. Harry's anger is almost tangible, and he looks destroyed.

He starts pacing the room and says harshly, "You bitch. I can't believe you slept with someone else when we were together and I was camping with our son. You slept with another person and not just anyone, a woman, in our bed. How could you Tina? No wonder you rejected me when I came home. What's the matter, was I too manly for you?"

I can understand his anger and feel a little scared by it but he needs to get this out because we can't move on unless he knows everything.

I say nothing and he continues to pace around the room before suddenly stopping and then heading towards the door. As I run after him, I call out, "Wait, where are you going? We need to talk about this… Harry, please!"

Suddenly, he stops and as he turns around, the look he shoots me makes me shrivel in self-disgust. He hates me. It's there in his eyes and on the sneer on his lips. Then he spits out, "Goodbye Tina."

33

Racing after him, I grab hold of his arm and pull him back, crying, "Please, Harry, we can talk about this and work it out."

Pushing me away, he snarls, "You know, Tina, I would have done anything for you once. I moved the earth to get you everything you ever wanted. I tried to be the perfect partner and father because I loved you more than anything. I worked every hour I could, so you didn't have to. I tried to treat you how I thought a woman would want to be treated and yet I got nothing back. I tried so hard to make you love me but it was never enough. Then you wanted another baby, and it didn't happen. You made me feel like a failure. I could see it in your eyes. You blamed me and that hurt the most. Then, when it turned out to be you with the problem, I tried to support you the best way I could. Then you found Isabel and started going on about surrogacy and I knew I had to put a stop to this. You weren't having any of it though, were you? You had to keep on pushing me and so you only have yourself to blame for what happened."

I stare at him in confusion. "I never knew. You never told me you felt like that."

He hisses, "I tried, but you never listened. You were so wrapped up in this weird crisis you were having, I didn't know what to do. Well, just so you know, somebody else tried to make me see things from your perspective. They tried to make me see that you were grieving and to give you space. They listened to my fears and helped me through a terrible time. They gave me support and comfort and tried to make me a better partner to you by suggesting things I could do to help you through."

I whisper, "Karen?"

He shakes his head angrily. "Isabel. Isabel, the woman you pushed me towards so I would agree to your demands. The woman responsible for putting that idea in your head and the woman whose name was never far from your lips."

Shaking my head, I say in a whisper, "Isabel, helped you?"

He nods. "Yes, and not just me. She helped your son too. When Jamie was crying at school, she spoke to him on several occasions. She tried to explain the situation and told him we both loved him and he would always be our number one priority. She called me when he broke down in class and she helped me talk it through with him. You see, Isabel was there when you were not and just obsessing over her. Then once again, the one person Jamie was relying on to help him through, was leaving him."

I shake my head sadly and say in a small voice, "I never knew. Why didn't I know? You both should have told me."

Suddenly, I feel angry as I think about their cosy chats and meetings with my son. Why wasn't I told?

My eyes flash as I shout, "How dare you?"

He looks surprised. "What?"

"Do all of that behind my back. I should have been informed."

Harry sneers. "What, that you were the problem in all our lives?"

He laughs dully, "Yes, you, Tina. The common denominator in all the shit in our lives is you. Now you've just decided that because Isabel doesn't want you, good old Harry will. She made it clear she wanted nothing to do with you, so you thought you could butter me up with my favourite meal and make me an offer you thought I'd seize with both hands. Well, the answer to your question is, No! I don't want to marry you and I won't be coming home. I'm leaving to take the job in Milton Keynes and will pay you an agreed amount to care for Jamie, with a bit over for yourself until you find a job. All of this, everything that's happened, is because of you, Tina. Just remember that."

He turns to leave and I pull him back. "Please Harry, you can't just leave like this, we need to talk about things, we can get through this."

Suddenly, his face softens and I catch my breath. He nods and pushes me back into the house and into the kitchen. Taking me in his arms, he pulls me tightly to him and says softly, "You know, I would have done anything for you once, babe. You were my world, and I loved you so much. I know you've been ill; I understand that. Maybe I'm not being supportive and have taken things too far."

My heart lifts as I hear his words. I knew he would come around. I feel it. I know him and Harry is coming back to me. It's in the soft tone to his voice and the comforting way he is holding me in his arms.

He whispers, "I just want you to know that I don't blame you in all this. You were ill and I should have recognised it and got you the help you needed. I suppose I was in denial but I couldn't cope. Promise me you'll get the help you need. I'll pay for it so don't worry about the cost."

I sob on his chest. "I will, I promise I'll get help. I just want everything back the way it was. I want you, Harry and I know that now. I should never have driven you away."

Pulling back, he smiles sadly. "Don't you think that if things were right it wouldn't have been so easy. Maybe it's for the best. We can both move on and be happier for it. You know, I'll always be your friend though, I promise you that at least."

I can't help the tears fall as he says gently, "Shall I call Karen, to come and sit with you?"

I hang onto him tightly, "I want you Harry, not Karen, just you. Please don't leave me."

I see the tears in his eyes as he gently pushes me away and says in a broken voice, "I must. I'm sorry babe, I'll call Karen on my out."

I watch Harry walk away and he takes my heart with him. All I am left with is a sense of loss and failure. How could I have taken him for granted and not seen the riches I already had with him? I've messed everything up and now the only hope I've got is that I can pull myself together and prove to him that I'm worth coming back for.

I hear the car move away and press my face against the window, as I watch the taillights disappear in the distance. Harry is gone and I have nobody to blame but myself.

34

ISABEL

As I pack up the last of my things, I think about my meeting with Karen earlier today. It was the right thing to do. I know that and the relief in her eyes told me I had done the right thing.

Smiling to myself, I reach for my phone and scroll to the photos. As the image flashes on the screen, I feel my heart harden. Yes, it was the right thing to do.

As I look at the photo, I've always had of Eddie and myself, I see the likeness. Eddie was clean shaven; Tom has a beard. Eddie's hair was shorter and his expression more confident. His arm is around my shoulders and I can see the watch glinting at the camera. Then I see the same shirt that I saw Tom wearing on the day of the barbeque and I smile to myself. Yes, Tom was Eddie, he always was. I always had this photograph, and I lied to Karen. I wanted to see if Tom regained his memory after that night he was attacked. I knew one day he would recognise me and it would all come out. Then things happened, and it ceased to matter anymore.

The key turns in the lock and I look up with a smile on my face that quickly fades when I see the expression on his face. As he heads inside, I feel the nerves flutter inside as Harry sits down wearily and says, "I couldn't tell her."

Moving across, I kneel before him and take his hands in mine. "I understand."

Shaking his head, he says tightly, "I need to know what happened with Tina, Isabel."

I feel my face fall and know she told him. I suppose I knew it would come out, but I didn't want anything to spoil what was growing so fast between us.

Moving to the seat on the other side facing him, I say sadly, "Tina had a few too many drinks. It wasn't unusual because she was hurting so badly. I just wanted to be a friend to her, you know, make things a little better for her. We had a lovely evening, and I told her I wanted to head home when she suggested a wine bar. Instead, she offered to make me a coffee at her house and I didn't think it would matter as I was dropping her off, anyway. Well, she was so sad and I didn't want to leave her, so I agreed to stay the night."

I almost can't look at Harry's face as I whisper, "I slept with her because I felt sorry for her. I didn't mean it to happen and when I woke up, I was mortified. I've never kissed another woman, and I didn't want to. The trouble is, Tina was quite forceful, and I didn't feel as if I had a choice."

Harry shouts, "She forced you?"

Wincing, I shake my head. "Sort of. I was so afraid because she was the only friend I had. I didn't want her to push me away, so well - I just let her."

I start to cry and Harry crosses the room and takes me in his arms, stroking the back of my head as he pulls me close. "It's ok, darling, I'm sorry to ask."

I feel weak as I lean against him for support and he whispers, "I understand. It must have been difficult for you and I want you to know I still love you."

Leaning back, I say roughly, "It was before you and I, well... you know."

He smiles sweetly. "It's fine, you don't have to say another word. It explains a lot though."

"What?"

"The reason why you wanted to move in with me so quickly and change your phone. You know, you could have told me you were going sick to escape from my ex. I would have helped if I'd known."

Burying my face in his chest, I feel my heart racing as I say softly, "I'm sorry, Harry, I should have told you. No more secrets from now on."

He lowers his lips to mine and says gruffly, "I love you Isabel."

My eyes fill with happy tears as I whisper, "I love you too, Harry."

As we kiss, I feel as if I've made it home at last. Everything that's happened in the last year, with Eddie, Tom, Karen and Tina has led me to this point. Harry and I have a future together in Milton Keynes and Jamie too. I love him like my own son and we will do everything we can to make a happy home for him. I feel a little guilty about Tina but all is fair in love and war and she didn't deserve Harry. She had her chance, and she blew it and I was only too happy to take him away from her.

As I pull away, Harry smiles lovingly. "You know, I can't wait to start my life with you."

Nodding, I pat my stomach and say in a whisper, "When will you tell Tina about the baby?"

He pulls me close and says softly, "When she's better and able to deal with it. Now isn't the time, which is why it's best we move away."

"But Jamie?"

He shakes his head sadly. "We will have to keep it from him for a few months. I don't like doing it but I'm not going to make things worse until she gets better. It's a difficult one."

Then he smiles and says brightly, "Anyway, we will deal with that when we have to. What we need now are food and an early night. We have an early start tomorrow and I can't wait to leave this place."

As I head to the kitchen, I have a huge smile on my face. Yes, it won't be an easy ride but we will take the journey as a team. I didn't intend to steal Harry but fate had a hand in it and here we are. Tina will be fine once the dust settles and she gets used to the idea. Jamie will have a brother or sister and belong to two families who love him very much.

As I stir the pot, I hum a happy tune. Family, after all, is everything.

35
KAREN

The blue lights flash as the police car crawls along the street. I wonder where they are destined to stop because this time, I know it's not us. Tom and Jack are playing on the computer upstairs, so I look with curiosity as the car edges along the street.

I hope it's not Tina. It took me most of the night to comfort her after Harry left. My heart ached for her when she told me he was leaving. I'd heard a rumour he was seeing someone else but hoped it was just malicious gossip. I still hope it is because more than anything, I want the two of them to get back together and life back to what it was, for all their sakes.

The clock chimes 7 pm and my heart stills as the car parks in a space outside in the road. I feel it thumping hard as I watch the two officers exit the car and start walking. They're coming this way but may pass. It could be Mrs Ironside next door, maybe her husband has had an accident, or worse.

Then in my heart, I already know as they stop outside our front gate and start walking the short distance up the path. I say nothing and just open the door before they can ring the bell and say anxiously, "May I help you?"

The officer's look uncomfortable and I wonder if it's my parents. Have they had an accident? My heart beats wildly as I wait for their words to find me, as I imagine every scenario possible in those brief seconds before they speak.

The officer says, "Does a Tom Mahoney live here?"

The blood freezes in my veins as I nod and call, "Tom, can you come here for a minute?"

He shouts down the stairs, "Can't it wait, I'm close to level 4?"

I smile nervously at the officers and say, "No, it can't I'm afraid."

I wince as he curses and then we hear his footsteps thumping on the ceiling above and he appears at the top of the stairs.

I think I'll never forget the look on his face as he comes down them. He looks devastated.

Before he even addresses the officers, he says quickly, "Go and sit with Jack. I'll come and find you later."

"But…"

He says harshly, "Now."

Feeling confused, I head upstairs to keep Jack occupied while he speaks to the officers and know in my heart that something bad has happened.

Jack looks up as I enter and I smile shakily, "Sorry, honey. Daddy has some business to sort out and asked if I'd take his place."

I don't miss the disappointment on Jack's face as he groans, "You're nowhere near as good as he is."

Rolling my eyes, I pretend to be hurt. "Thanks, Jack, you know how to make your mum feel great."

He shrugs and carries on with his game but I can't concentrate on anything else other than what may be happening downstairs.

It must only be ten minutes later when Tom pokes his head around the door and says apologetically, "I've got to go out, I won't be long."

Jack nods and carries on with his game and I follow him out of the room, whispering, "What is it, Tom? Are you in some kind of trouble?"

He shakes his head and looks upset. "I'm sorry, Karen, for everything. Listen, let me deal with the police and when I get back, we'll talk then."

"But…"

He shakes his head. "Not now. I won't be long."

I stand at the top of the stairs and watch as Tom grabs his coat and accompanies the officers outside. The looks on all of their faces are grave and whatever has happened is serious because when Tom looked at me, I could see it in his eyes. Something is worrying him and when he gets back, I'm not sure if I want to hear what it is.

The phone rings interrupting my thoughts and I grab it quickly. "Yes?"

"Karen, what's happening, are Tom and Jack ok?"

"Yes, fine...um, Tom had to go with them but I don't know why."

Tina says firmly, "I'm coming over."

Before I can tell her not to, the line is cut and I stand waiting to give an explanation on something I don't know the first thing about.

The next knock on the door is Tina's, and she brings Jamie with her who true to form shoots past me straight upstairs.

I smile at her gratefully as she says, "There, that should keep them occupied while we talk about this."

We head into the kitchen for the all healing cup of tea and she says, "Why do the police want to speak to Tom?"

I say in a worried voice, "I don't know. He told me he would tell me when he returned. I'm scared though, Tina. What if he's done something?"

"Like what?" She laughs in disbelief.

Shrugging, I face her with trepidation. "There is something, I can feel it. I suppose I've always known there is but could never put my finger on it."

She looks confused. "What do you mean?"

Sitting down, I put my head in my hands. "He's been different, Tina. Ever since the night he was mugged, he seemed different."

"In what way?"

"I don't know, better I suppose. He was like the old Tom I married. Kind, attentive, loving, all the things he lost sight of over the years. I thought maybe the trauma had made him re-evaluate things but what if something else happened that night that changed him? Maybe he did something so terrible it altered him forever."

Tina laughs in disbelief. "Tom - do something terrible. Never. He may have been a complete asshole back then, but he was never... well, you know... dangerous."

Despite myself, I laugh. "Dangerous?"

She giggles. "The way you're talking, it's as if you think he murdered someone. No, whatever this is, Tom will have a rational explanation. Just make sure you text me when you know what it is because I won't sleep a wink until I know."

I look at her in concern. "How are things, have you got over the shock yet?"

I see the pain in her eyes as she shakes her head sadly. "It's hard, Karen. I thought things would get back to normal but they never will be again. It's only been less than a week since Harry left but I miss him so much it hurts. Do you think he'll ever come back to me?"

I try to reassure her even though I can't think straight. "Of course, he will. Just give him time and he'll soon realise what he's missing."

As we sit contemplating the mess our lives have fallen into, we don't notice the time until Jack comes down and says wearily, "Can Jamie stay tonight?"

Looking at the clock, I jump up and shake my head. "Goodness is that the time. Maybe we should let Tina and Jamie head home, you do have school in the morning, after all."

Jack groans and Tina shouts, "Jamie, home!"

As Jamie thunders downstairs, Tina hugs me and whispers, "It will all be fine. I just know it."

I smile shakily but know in my heart things will never be the same again.

36
TOM & EDDIE

As I stand waiting, I think my life flashes before my eyes. I always knew I would be standing here one day. In my heart, I've always known because even from an early age I knew we were so different, despite looking identical.

The police officer pulls back the sheet and I see him. Cold, lifeless and unfeeling. In death, as he was in life. My twin brother.

I nod and the officer says sympathetically, "Do you need more time?"

Shaking my head, I turn away. "No - thank you."

The officer replaces the sheet and I follow him out of the mortuary. I don't look back and any feelings I may ever have had for that man lying dead on the slab, died that night.

The officer takes me to a room and pushes a Styrofoam cup of tea in my direction and says sympathetically, "I'm sorry for your loss."

As I sample the hot tea, I just nod. "Thank you."

He sits awkwardly and pushes a box towards me. "These are all the possessions we found of his. We thought you would want them."

As I look at the box, I shake my head and say sadly, "Not much to show for a life, is it?"

"No, I don't suppose it is."

The officer clears his throat. "I expect you have many questions."

Reaching out, I draw the box towards me and say dully, "What was the cause of death?"

"Drowning. He left a note and the items of clothes that are in the box before you. His wallet gave us his identity enabling us to trace you, although it took a little time to find him after he was reported missing."

I look at him in surprise. "Who reported it?"

"An Isabel Rawlins, his fiancée."

I feel the anger flooding through me as I think of my brother with Isabel. He was a bastard to the end, and it's no wonder she came looking for him.

The officer shakes his head. "Maybe I shouldn't say it but it appears as if she had a lucky escape."

As I raise my eyes to his, he says nervously, "I'm sorry, but it appears your brother was into all sorts of dodgy dealings. He rented a flat that he hardly ever stayed in. We think he just used it to secure credit cards and loans because he is leaving a shitload of debt behind him. I'm not surprised he killed himself when you think about who he owed money to."

"Who?"

"Known criminals who run illegal gambling syndicates. They're into all kinds, prostitution, pornography and illegal trafficking not to mention drugs. If your brother owed them money, he didn't have long to live."

I say gruffly, "Do you think they had a hand in his death?"

The officer shakes his head. "No. I doubt it because he's better off to them alive. They won't get anything now he's dead, it's not their style. No, it's more likely he took the easy way out rather than be drafted into their world. Maybe he did it to protect his girlfriend, although why he never went to her family for help, I'll never know."

I stare at him in surprise. "Her family? Why, what could they have done to help him?"

Leaning forward, the officer whispers, "The Rawlins family are just as corrupt, if not more so. No other crime family would go against them, it wouldn't be worth the trouble. If your brother had gone to them with his problems, they would have protected him because to them, family is everything."

His words surprise me because I never thought of Isabel being some sort of mafia princess. She just doesn't look the type.

I turn to the officer and say dully, "May I leave now, shall I arrange for the undertakers to collect his body?"

The officer nods. "Of course. We aren't treating his death as suspicious, so you are free to bury him, the poor soul."

As I shake his hand, I smile gratefully. "Thank you. We'll be in touch when I've arranged an undertaker."

The officer accompanies me to the door and shakes his head. "You know, despite your beard, you're the spitting image of each other. Uncanny really."

I smile. "That's twins for you, especially identical ones. However, we are very different in personality, one good, one not so."

I walk away with the officer's laughter ringing in my ears. Yes, Tom Mahoney was a very different man to Edward Mahoney which is why he asked for my help on that fateful night.

I get a cab back from the station and think about the last time I saw my brother. I had just returned from a long trip overseas and was desperate for some sleep in a comfortable bed. I just didn't expect to find my brother in it with some woman he picked up from the Internet. As I close my eyes it all comes flooding back.

37

The woman screams as I flick on the light and stare in surprise at the two figures naked in my bed.

I roar, "What the hell is going on?"

His laughter mocks me as he rolls off the woman and smirks. "Good to see you, bro. Fancy sharing, it wouldn't be the first time."

The woman shrieks and I say angrily, "Get out, both of you."

I watch as she jumps from the bed, gathering up her clothes, shouting, "Fucking perverts! I'm going to report you to the dating service for this, creep."

My brother just laughs like a madman as she pushes past me and it's not until the door slams that I snarl, "That includes you too, get out!"

He shrugs and leaves the bed, totally naked and stretches with contentment. "It's a shame you interrupted that. She was one of my more adventurous partners."

Shaking my head, I snarl, "I don't give a fuck about your sex life. I just want to sleep in my own bed and forget I've even got a brother."

I don't miss the look in his eyes as he pulls on his jeans and my sixth sense kicks in. "What's that look for?"

He looks worried which instantly makes me *very* worried. "Listen, bro, I think I need to warn you about something."

"What?"

He sits on the side of the bed and says in a strangely apologetic voice, "I didn't mean for this to happen?"

The alarm bells ring as I say, "What, you're in trouble again, aren't you?"

Nodding, he raises his eyes to mine and I see the torment in them. "I'm sorry, Eddie, I've kind of got you into something you may not easily get out of."

My tiredness is instantly cured as I sit on the chair by the wall and say grimly, "Then tell me."

He shrugs. "Listen, you know how I've always loved to gamble, maybe a bit too much."

I nod. "Well. I may have gone a little far and used your identity to take out a few credit cards and loans in your absence."

I take a deep breath. "How much do you… I… owe?"

"£50,000."

"What the…?"

He nods looking uncomfortable. "Yes, I'm sorry to say I owe it to some loan sharks who aren't the sort of guys you want to owe anything to."

I snarl, "You'd better have the money to pay them back even if you have to sell your house. Anyway, does your wife know about this, you and your sordid life of whores and gambling?"

He looks up angrily. "It's none of her damned business, stupid cow. I should have divorced the bitch a long time ago, but she was useful."

I explode. "Useful. Your own fucking wife and mother of your child is … useful!"

He shrugs. "As I said, I should have divorced her years ago. Anyway, I'm not as bad as you think and I have a plan but I need your help."

"If you think I'm having anything to do with this, you're mistaken."

"You will because actually it's not me they're after - it's you."

I don't hear anymore and just lunge at my brother. I know whatever he's done is bad for me and I'm going to hurt him - big time. I'm not sure how long we fight for but years of resentment, anger and frustration boil over and we fight like two boxers in the ring. It's only when we sit broken and bleeding on the ground that I say hoarsely, "Tell me your plan and don't leave anything out."

He spits blood on his hand and says roughly, "I need to disappear and when I say me, I mean *you*, Edward Mahoney."

"You used my fucking name!"

He laughs bitterly. "Not exactly. I used Eddie Butler."

I shake my head in disbelief. "You used our grandfather's name, why?"

"Because I hated him and thought it would be fun to use his name in vain. I gambled, drank and slept with more women than you've ever seen in your miserable life and I did it as him. He had a good time, so don't feel sorry for him."

I feel so angry it hurts and long to punch him until his eyes close for good and then he laughs and says dully, "It was easy. These women are desperate and believe anything you tell them. I had a lot of fun being Eddie Butler but I needed Edward Mahoney to get the money. The trouble is, now Eddie Butler is a wanted man and it won't be long before they connect him to you. You aren't safe anymore so need to disappear, as do I."

"You, why do you need to disappear?"

"Because I'm leaving. I have a villa in Spain I bought with my winnings and I'm not prepared to give it to them. I also want out of my marriage but can't spare the time or trouble to battle it out in court and see that bitch Karen getting all my money."

"But you have a son, what about him?"

He laughs bitterly, "So she says. You know, I never wanted him. I told her I didn't want kids, and she tricked me into it. It just shows what a bitch she is and who knows he probably isn't mine, anyway. No, I'm getting away from the whole shitstorm and you are going to take my place because it's the safest one for you."

I can't believe what I'm hearing and jump to my feet and he holds up his hand and says angrily, "Think about it before you go flying off the handle. You become me as I did you. It won't matter because Karen and I are on the rocks, anyway. Just pretend to be me for a few months and then divorce the bitch. Make sure you don't give her more than the bare minimum though. Meanwhile, I'll stage your – Eddie's suicide and leave a note so the gangs stop looking for me. Then I flee to Spain and live happily ever after under a new identity."

I snort, "You're delusional."

He laughs like a madman. "Oh no, brother, I have it all worked out. This way we both keep our lives, although very different ones. If you become me, it means I can escape without the problem of my marriage getting in the way. You may have a few months of being me but then you can go off to another one of those countries you like to visit and lose yourself for years on end. Karen and Jack live happily ever after without me in their lives and everyone's happy."

I just stare at him in total shock. "You bastard."

Groaning, he stands and shrugs. "I never pretended otherwise. Anyway, when you think about it, you'll know it's the only way if you value your own life."

I say angrily, "I'll go to the police and tell them everything."

He actually smiles and then says lightly, "If you like, although I'm sure when I deny everything and have the back up of my loving family against the word of a loner with no friends and family of his own, I wouldn't place any bets on who they'll believe."

"But I can prove I was out of the country."

Tom shrugs. "No, you can't because I have been you all the time you were away. We both know you have no proof because you bummed your way around the world with only the bare essentials. You know, Edward, you made it easy for me. The fact you turned your back on society to find yourself by backpacking around the world with nothing, earning your money as you went, made this all a lot easier for me. You see, no one knew you had gone and there are no records of Edward Mahoney travelling anywhere. If you do happen to find someone to back up your story, good luck with that because you'll be dead before they speak up. All the records show that Edward Mahoney left the army and went mad. You, of course, did so literally by going on some kind of self-imposed exile, while I did it in a much more satisfying way. So, you see one day you will thank me, bro, because I am giving you an identity and a life, it's just up to you what you do with it."

Once again, I look at him with so much hatred I can't speak. He stares at me with pity in his eyes and says, "You know it's the only way. You become me and I get out of Dodge."

As I watch my brother get dressed, I don't even register the state I'm in. Both of us are bruised, bleeding and broken and our lives will never be the same again. As I sit watching him, I make a vow to myself. I'll go along with his plan for his family's sake only. The thought of his son finding out what a scumbag his father is fills me with horror. I picture them standing over his grave mourning a life that wasn't worth a single shed tear because if the criminals don't get my brother, I will.

38

TOM & KAREN

I'm not sure what I'm going to tell Karen, if anything. A thousand thoughts have spun through my head as I make the journey home.

The night I became Tom Mahoney my life changed – for the better. I never intended on falling in love with my brother's wife and son but over the months it became impossible not to. I suppose I overcompensated for his lack of feeling and tried to make up for it. However, I soon stopped trying something that came naturally.

So, he was right; I did end up thanking him because he gave me my life back. When I left the army, I was broken. I had seen and done things no man should ever have in his memory and I needed to get away. I think I went a little crazy and my trip around the world was to save my sanity. I volunteered and tried to give back something to society that I feel I took when I remember the men that fell in the name of our country.

So, Edward Mahoney has now died forever and seeing my brother today has put my mind at rest. He won't be back to blow my cover and claim what I have grown to love. We are now free to live our lives as we mean to, together, in love and as a family. What did that officer say, family is everything? That sentence resonated with me because it is. Family *is* everything and I will protect mine to the death.

As soon as I return home, I see Karen anxiously waiting at the door. I don't miss the relief in her eyes as I draw her close and kiss her with everything I've got. Then I take her hand and lead her to the couch and say gently, "I have something to tell you."

When Tom finally falls asleep in my arms, I think about what he told me. I still can't believe he had a brother, a twin brother at that. However, once he told me what his brother was like, I kind of understood why he kept him from me. My thoughts turn to Isabel and I feel sad for her. She wasn't wrong when she thought Tom was Eddie. They looked the same and it must have been a shock to see him. However, she doesn't know the full story.

My heart broke when Tom told me how Eddie had fallen into debt and despair. He had tried to help him without involving us, which is why the money had been tight for so long before that fateful night. He told me he wasn't mugged, and that Eddie had approached him as he got off the train. Things grew heated and they had a huge fight. Tom told him he never wanted to see him again and offered him money to go abroad to escape the people he owed money to. He even gave him his watch to sell but Eddie didn't listen and took his own life.

My heart broke for my husband as he spoke of his brother. How he had once loved him so hard it hurt and now, he just felt an emptiness where the bond used to be. Eddie took his own life to escape his problems and left Isabel grieving for a man who didn't exist.

Thinking about Isabel, I hope she's happy where she is. It's funny how I always thought of her as a husband thief. I always thought she had her sights set on mine. How wrong I turned out to be.

Epilogue
ISABEL

It's becoming difficult to walk with the huge baby inside me but I had to come. Closure is needed, and this is the place I will get it.

Luckily, Harry is spending the weekend with Jamie at Center Parcs and so, I have joined my father and brother to pay a very special visit to an old acquaintance.

"Are you ok babe?"

I smile at my father and squeeze his hand tightly. "I'll be fine when this is over."

My brother snarls, "My only regret was it was over so quickly."

My father laughs softly as we stand hand in hand as one family and look at the gravestone.

Edward Mahoney

A brave soldier

Fallen but not forgotten

We share a look and then I feel my baby kick. Harry's baby. The man I never knew I'd find while looking for another. He is everything to me and I couldn't love him more. My husband.

We married a few months ago in Antigua, witnessed by my family. The family Eddie never wanted to meet and the cause of his ultimate downfall.

When I told my father what had happened, he was angry. He traced Eddie Butler to Edward Mahoney and through his contacts they discovered he had fled to Spain after faking his own suicide. He had just a few short months thinking he had escaped when my brother found him and brought him home.

I was called back to identify him and I will never forget the look in his eyes as he called me a whore in front of my own family. He had no remorse, no guilt and no conscience so it was easy. I watched my father hold his head under the water as my brother held him down. His body struggled, and I enjoyed every minute of it as I remembered the things he made me do to him.

It seems that you'll do anything for love as I discovered when I let Tina maul me that night. I always knew it would come out, and it was the final nail in her relationship with Harry. By then I'd hooked him on my line and he wasn't going anywhere. Tina was out of the picture and I rode off into the sunset with her family. I don't feel guilty though because everyone knows family is everything, as the little boy growing inside me is about to find out. We look after our family – the Rawlins and now Harry and Jamie are part of that family and if anything threatens our future happiness – well, that will be their last mistake.

I smile happily as I look at the gravestone and whisper, "Thank you, daddy, thank you, Sean."

They each squeeze my hand and we turn away, as I savour the moment. Justice was done, and it's time to move on leaving the dirt in the ground where it belongs.

As we walk away, I wonder if Karen ever found out her husband swapped identities. In a way, I hope she didn't because the brother she ended up with was the better one. If I hadn't followed him home, I would never have made the connection.

Maybe I'll tell her one day, maybe I won't. Either way, she'll be happier with Tom number 2 because Tom number one, deserved all he got.

Once again, my baby kicks and my father laughs softly. "A true Rawlins that one. He'll come out fighting, you mark my words."

Yes, my baby's going to discover what family means because above everything, he's a Rawlins and if you upset one of us, you pay with your life.

THE END

Thank you for reading The Husband Thief. If you have enjoyed the story, I would be so grateful if you could post a review on Amazon. It really helps other readers when deciding what to read and means everything to the Author who wrote it.

Connect with me on Facebook

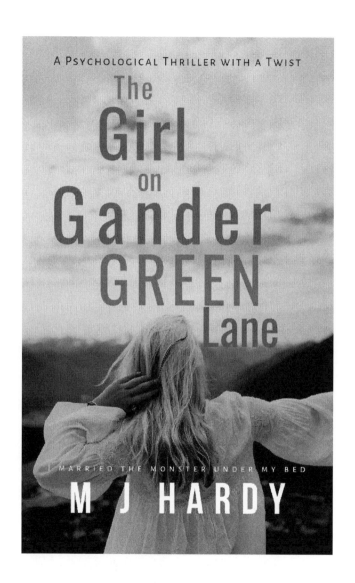

A PSYCHOLOGICAL THRILLER WITH A TWIST

The
Girl
on
Gander
GREEN
Lane

I MARRIED THE MONSTER UNDER MY BED

M J HARDY

243

A Chilling Psychological Thriller with a Twist.

When a perfect marriage, the perfect husband and perfect life is nothing but an illusion.

Then one night, the nightmare reveals itself.

Sarah Standon is living the dream, at least that's what everyone tells her.
She is the wife of a successful solicitor who looks like a movie star.
They live a Stepford existence and appear to have it all.
But then one fateful night, everything changes.
A terrible accident leaves Sarah alone to deal with a situation so frightening that she starts to question her grip on reality.
Her perfect life has been exposed as the lie it always was and she loses everything.

She thought that was the worst that could happen.

She was wrong.

Made in the USA
Coppell, TX
29 December 2019

13851613R00143